ARMED AND DANGEROUS

Price dropped on Cronin, knees driving savagely into the man's belly, and he hit him on the face, rocking his head to one side and then the other. Rose screamed, "Get off!" and prodded him in the back with the muzzle of her shotgun. "Get off him, damn you!"

Cronin wasn't knocked cold, but as Price got to his feet and backed away Cronin showed no inclination to get up. Rose kept the shotgun pointed at Price. She was crying, tears running down her face. "Get up, Walt." She wiped a dirty sleeve across her face. "You can whip him, Walt. Get up."

Cronin raised himself on one elbow and fell back. Blood ran down his face from his nose and his mouth and made red streaks on his chin and neck. He said through bruised lips, "I'm licked."

"Want me to shoot his God-damned head off?" Rose demanded. "I can do it."

WAYNE D. OVERHOLSER

**Twice Winner of the Spur Award
and Winner of
The Lifetime Achievement Award from
The Western Writers of America**

WAYNE D. OVERHOLSER

THE LONE DEPUTY

LEISURE BOOKS NEW YORK CITY

A LEISURE BOOK ®

December, 1991

Published by special arrangement with MACMILLAN PUBLISH-ING COMPANY, a division of Macmillan, Inc.

Dorchester Publishing Co., Inc.
276 Fifth Avenue
New York, NY 10001

For further information, contact: Macmillan Publishing Co., a division of Macmillan Inc., 866 Third Avenue, New York, NY 10022

Chapter 1

PRICE REGAN DIMLY HEARD THE TAP ON HIS DOOR, THEN turned over, invisible hands pulling him back into the deep pit of sleep. The tap came again, and he buried his head under his pillow. The third time it was sharp and angry, and he sat up, calling, "All right, all right."

He pulled on his pants, yawning. The moment he opened the door, Laura Madden slipped into the room. He reached for her to push her back into the hall, but she whirled away from him.

"You can't come in here," he said angrily. "Get out and let me dress."

"Shut the door, Grumpy," she said. "Of course I can come in here. We're getting married next week, aren't we?"

He closed the door and leaned against it, looking at her. She was a slender, high-spirited girl not quite nineteen. As far as he was concerned, she was the prettiest girl in the world, with dark blue eyes and blonde hair that held a rebellious curl, and he knew he was a lucky man to have won her love. Still, he wished she was less girl and more woman. When she was in one of her gay and reckless moods as she was now, he simply didn't know how to cope with her.

"I'm just the groom," he said, "but seems like I ought to be told the date of the wedding."

She laughed, wrinkling her nose at him. "I just told you." She assumed an expression of mock gravity. "I'm ashamed of you, Price. Town Marshal of Saddle Rock and Deputy Sheriff of the west end of Tremaine County, and you're still in bed at seven o'clock Saturday morning. How are you going to earn the baby a shirt when you're that lazy?"

"Nobody tells me anything," he groaned. "I didn't know we had a baby who needed a shirt. Now will you get out of here and . . ."

"No, I won't." She crossed the room and kissed him. "Price, Daddy wants to see you first thing this morning."

That was Barry Madden for you. He was the banker, so you went to see him. He never came to see you. Price said, "Funny how good things and bad things get all mixed up. You're good and I get you for a wife, but I've got to take Barry Madden for a father-in-law."

"That's not fair," she cried. "Daddy's used to having people come . . ."

"He can get unused to it," Price said. "He knows where to find me."

She looked at him, her red lips parted at the center. "Please, Price," she said softly. "You say we can't get married because you won't let me live in your hotel room, and you won't live in Daddy's house. Well, last night we heard the Bryce house was for sale."

So that was it. Barry Madden would buy a house and give it to them for a wedding present, but it wouldn't be free to Price Regan. There was bound to be a joker in the deal. Nothing that Barry Madden gave away was ever free.

She said, "Please, Price."

He knew he had to go. He said, "All right, I'll see him."

She kissed him again. "We really can get married next week if Daddy buys the house for us." She stepped past him and put a hand on the doorknob, then she looked back to him, her face troubled. "Be careful, Price. Cole Weston stayed in town last night."

"Then Pete Nance is here, too," Price said. "Curly Blue, too, chances are."

"I suppose they are," she said. "You will be careful, won't you?"

He laughed. "I'm not the careful kind. It's Weston and his hard cases who had better be careful."

"Oh, you're impossible," she said, and went out, slamming the door.

He shaved and finished dressing, thinking that their chance of getting married next week was a mighty slim one. He had been using the lack of a house as an excuse for postponing their marriage, but it wasn't the real reason.

A bitter wind was blowing across the west end of Tremaine County, a wind that carried the seeds of tragedy, of passion and greed and death. Cole Weston was the man who was blowing up that wind, but until it had blown itself out and Weston's wings were clipped, Price couldn't marry Laura. It was not a thing he could explain to her, so he hadn't tried.

In many ways Price Regan was a tough and formidable man. He had been a deputy for four years, and he was a good one. If he hadn't been, Sheriff Ralph Carew would never have sent him here. To Price the law was something more than words; it was an ideal, an instrument by which justice could be handed down in any situation.

At least that was the way Ralph Carew believed it should be, and he had given that belief to Price Regan, but justice was a term that meant nothing to Cole Weston and Barry Madden. The world was full of men of their caliber, and in some places they would have been incapable of doing harm; but put one of them in a bank and let the other one own the biggest spread in the country, and they were in position to raise hell and prop it up with a stick.

When Price went downstairs to the hotel dining room for breakfast, he looked around for Weston, expecting to see him, but the cattleman wasn't in sight. The more Price thought about it, the more he was convinced that there was a connection between Weston's presence in town and Madden's request to come to the bank. The two of them worked together, and Price doubted that Madden ever took a step without consulting Weston.

After Price finished breakfast and crossed the street to the bank, he still had not seen Weston or any of his men. It was several minutes before nine, the bank's opening time, so Price had to knock on the door.

Cranky old John Ramey unlocked the door and started to tell Price in a sulfuric tone that he could come back when the bank was open for business, but Price pushed past him into the room.

"Shut up, John," Price said amiably. "Someday you're going to burn your tongue right off at the end, and I won't be one damned bit sorry."

He walked through the gate at the end of the counter and went on to the private office in the back. Here Barry Madden smoked and dreamed and schemed while John Ramey sat on a tall stool with his green eyeshade on his forehead and worked on the books or waited on customers in the teller's cage. John's salary was less than half what it should have been, but he never complained. He liked to sit in the seat of the mighty, Price thought. He liked to feel important.

So John Ramey did the hard work that it took to keep the bank solvent, and that left Barry Madden free to do his smoking and dreaming and scheming. It was the scheming, Price knew, that had brought him here this morning.

When Price knocked on the door, Madden said, "Come in." He sat at his mahogany desk, a few papers and a box of cigars in front of him. When he saw who it was, he rose, calling: "Come in, Price. Come on in, boy. I'm glad to see you."

Madden shook Price's hand, patted him on the back, and motioned for him to sit down. He offered the box of cigars, but Price shook his head and rolled a cigarette. Madden took a cigar and put it into his mouth, but didn't light it.

The banker was about forty, a widower who had lost his wife before Price came to Saddle Rock, and the result was that all the affection the man was capable of generating was fastened on Laura. Price knew Madden did not approve of him as a son-in-law, but as yet he had made no objection, following his habit of giving Laura anything she wanted he was capable of giving.

Madden leaned back in his chair, tucking the cold cigar into one corner of his mouth. He was a blocky man with a wide chin and high-bridged nose, and a synthetic affability which failed to disguise the desire to dominate which was so much a part of him.

"Well, son, you're a lucky man to have Laura's love," Madden said.

"I know I am," Price said.

"When do you plan to get married?"

"Laura said something about next week."

Madden tongued the cigar to the other side of his mouth. "She mentioned the Bryce house?" Price nodded, and Madden went on, "It was in my mind to buy it and give it to you as a wedding present."

"That's right generous," Price said, "but what's it going to cost me?"

Madden stared at him a moment, then slapped his desk with an open palm, shouting angrily, "Well, by God, that's a funny thing to say to your future father-in-law when he proposes to give you something!"

"No use of us trying to fool each other, Barry," Price said. "I don't like you because of the way you front for Cole Weston and the rest of the cowmen, and you don't like me because I make barely enough to live on and you've got some big ideas about Laura marrying money."

Madden glowered at Price a moment, then he said, "When are you going to throw away that star and take a job that'll make you a decent living?"

"You mean Weston needs another gunslinger beside Pete Nance?" Price shrugged. "I'll never take that kind of a job, Barry. Next year I'm going to run for sheriff. Ralph Carew's getting old and he wants me to have the star."

Madden drummed his fingertips on the desk for a moment. Then he said, "Carew could swing it for you on the other side of the mountains and I could do it here. And I will if you're smart."

"I'm not smart, Barry."

"I've wondered." Madden got up and walked to a big map of Tremaine County that hung on the wall. "Price, I sent for you this morning for just one reason. I want you to do your job." Madden pointed to the Singing Wind Range that bisected the county. "Here's a barrier that cuts us off from the east half of the county where most of the people live. Farmers." He said the word with evident distaste. "Ralph Carew is a farmer's sheriff."

"He'd be the first to admit it."

Madden put his finger on the mountain range as if he hadn't heard. "Here's Domino Pass, closed most of the year. Still closed even in June. Thirty miles to the county seat across the pass, but better than one hundred if you swing north around the mountains, so we're actually cut off from the rest of the county for the time the pass is closed. That makes you the law in this end of the county for more than half of each year."

Price nodded, still not sure what Madden was getting at.

"We're going to have our own county one of these days." Madden stabbed the town of Saddle Rock with a forefinger. "When we do, the county seat will be right here. I'll see to it that you're our first sheriff, and you won't have to take Laura away from home."

"It'll never be a county as long as Cole Weston and Red Sanders and the Mohawk boys run things." Price threw his cigarette stub into a spittoon and, getting up, walked to the map. He ran a finger down the line that was Elk River. "Barry, there's enough meadowland below town to give a living to a thousand people, if you and Weston would let them settle it. Someday they're going to come regardless. When they do, I'll see they are allowed to settle because the law will be on their side."

Madden wheeled away from Price and walked back to his desk. He stood there while he fought his temper. If it hadn't been for Laura, he would probably have ordered Price out of his office. No one, unless it was Cole Weston, talked to him that way. Here, Price knew, was the real difficulty between him on one hand and Madden and the cowmen on the other. The previous deputies had taken orders from them. Price Regan didn't, and he'd made it clear from the first.

Madden swung around. "I'll tell you what the Bryce house will cost you. Run Walt Cronin and his woman out of the country."

So that was it! Price should have expected it. He looked at the map. Five miles downriver from Saddle Rock Walt Cronin had a store and saloon that catered to the poverty-stricken settlers who squatted on Yellow Cat Creek that emptied into Elk River at that point.

The Yellow Cat divided the Mohawk boys' Broken Ring from Bridlebit that belonged to Red Sanders. On the other side of the river for miles to the south the country was claimed by the Rocking C, Cole Weston's spread.

How the settlers survived on a hardscrabble range like the Yellow Cat Valley was a mystery to Price, and the answer might lie in the gossip that was prevalent, that Cronin and the settlers consistently stole from the big ranches that surrounded them.

Price turned to the banker. "Barry, I've been out there

hunting for evidence, but I've never found any. When and if I do, I'll arrest Cronin and anyone else who's implicated. Until I do, I will not run Cronin anywhere."

Madden was breathing hard. "To hell with evidence!" he shouted. "You know what Cronin's doing. You let it go and there'll be a fight. The only way to stop it is to get rid of Cronin. If you don't, you'll lose both your job and your girl."

"You can take half of my job away from me," Price said, "but I'm not so sure about my girl. I guess that's up to her." He walked to the door and stopped to look back. "Barry, there's one thing you're forgetting. Cronin and the settlers are innocent until we get the evidence to prove they're guilty. If it's as bad as you think, why hasn't Weston or one of the others brought in some evidence?"

He went out and shut the door behind him, Madden glaring after him. He had just turned a potential enemy into an active one who would do everything in his power to turn Laura against him. Yet, as Price walked past John Ramey on his tall stool and went on out of the bank, he knew he would have said and done exactly as he had if he were given the opportunity to live these last few minutes over again.

When he thought back over the years, he knew how easy it would have been for him to have gone bad. Or at least to have become a hired gunslinger like Pete Nance. The difference was that Ralph Carew had taken enough interest in him to hire him as a deputy and teach him what it meant to be a lawman.

As he closed the bank door behind him, it occurred to him that if he were another Pete Nance he would not have asked Laura Madden to marry him, but that was a fine point her father could not understand.

Chapter 2

PRICE HAD FORGOTTEN ABOUT CURLY BLUE BEING IN TOWN with Cole Weston and Pete Nance, but he was reminded of it as he approached the livery stable. Blue stood in front of the archway, his hat shoved back on his forehead, hands jammed into his pants' pockets. He's drunk, Price thought, as Blue swayed a little on uncertain legs, his slack-lipped mouth holding a taunting grin.

In the year Price had been there, he had jailed Curly Blue for drunkenness and fighting more than any other three men in the west end of Tremaine County. He had usually treated him rough, and on at least two occasions had knocked him cold with his gun barrel before hauling him off to jail. Blue was a bad one by almost any standard, a brawler who had no honor, who fought without rules and who seemed to get pleasure from maiming a man after he had him whipped.

Neither Weston nor Nance was anywhere in sight, but Price suspected that both were watching. He knew he was headed for trouble when he was still thirty feet from Blue, and he was convinced that it was a put-up job and that Barry Madden had, by some prearranged signal, got word to Cole Weston that he had failed. Now Curly Blue was to do by force what Madden had been unable to do by bribery. Price wouldn't take orders, so now he was to take a beating, or maybe get killed.

"Howdy, Curly," Price said. "Aren't you drinking a little early today?"

"Hell no," Blue said. "I ain't drinking. I'm fighting. I aim to lick hell out of you."

"You'd better head for the Rocking C and sleep it off," Price said, "if you don't want to wind up in jail."

Blue spit contemptuously into the dust at Price's feet. He was a big man, taller and heavier than Price, and now that he was close, Price saw that his eyes were clear. *He wasn't drunk.* This was play acting that was typical of Cole Weston's scheming.

"You're a crook, Marshal." Blue waggled a finger at Price. "You figure to get on your horse and ride out to see your pal Cronin and talk about how you're gonna steal some more Rocking C cows. That's why I'm gonna lick you, Marshal. I'm just gonna lick hell out of you."

"Get out of the way, Curly, or—"

Price didn't have time to finish his sentence. Blue rushed him, a big fist swinging for his head. Someone on the street yelled, "Fight! fight!" and men rushed out of doorways to form a circle around Price and Blue in front of the livery stable. Price had no time to see who was there and who wasn't. He backed up and, turning, caught Blue on the side of the head with a hard right that jarred and hurt the cowboy.

Blue grunted and wheeled and came at Price again. Wickedness danced in his eyes, cold, calculating wickedness as if he were thinking of all the injuries he had suffered at Price's hands in the past and now he was going to square his account.

Price backed up again, ducking a roundhouse right, and slammed a punch through to Blue's nose, which flattened under his fist like an overripe tomato. The cowboy bellowed in pain, blood streaming down his face, and charged again.

Curly Blue knew only two ways to fight: to keep boring in until one of his club-like blows landed, or to get his arms around his enemy and drag him down into the dust. He'd butt with his head or use his elbows and knees, or gouge out a man's eyes with his thumbs. Knowing this, Price kept backing up, taking Blue's punches on his elbows or shoulders, or ducking them and countering with blows that stung but lacked the authority it took to end the fight.

Price had a fast pair of hands, and Ralph Carew had insisted that he learn to use them just as he had insisted Price learn to handle a gun. So now Price waited for the chance he was certain would come.

There was little noise from the crowd, and he wondered about that. The circle was fluid, moving back with Blue's headlong charges as Price gave ground, so he always had room. Cole Weston and Pete Nance would be in that circle somewhere, and the thought kept nagging Price that if he broke his right hand on Curly Blue's head, Nance would force a gun fight on him.

Blue's failure to close with Price goaded him into a kind of insane frenzy, and it was this frenzy which gave Price his opportunity. Blue missed one of his great swinging uppercuts, turning partly around and off balance. Price moved in swiftly and smoothly. He threw a right that caught Blue under the chin on his windpipe, then a left to the jaw, the sound of the second blow as solid as a butcher's cleaver on a quarter of beef.

Price stepped back, rubbing his knuckles as Blue went down in a curling fall and lay motionless in the dust, blood from his smashed nose making a scarlet mask on his battered face.

Price looked around at the circle of men. Max Harker, the storekeeper; Barney De Long, who owned the livery stable; and others he had learned to know reasonably well in the months he had been here, but Madden, he saw, was not here. As his gaze swung from one to the other of these men, it seemed to him they were neutral, yet he had a feeling they would have been his friends if they had not balanced their desire for friendship against the knowledge that to be Price Regan's friend was to be Cole Weston's enemy.

"Fun's over," Price said.

They broke up, Barney De Long disappearing into the livery stable, and it was then that Price saw Cole Weston and Pete Nance standing in the doorway. Price moved toward them, right hand close to the butt of his gun. A sudden dark anger took hold of him and he wished that Nance would make a wrong move, but he doubted that the gunman would. The fight with Blue had not gone the way Cole Weston had planned.

"He's your man, Cole," Price said. "Take him to the doc, then get him out of town or I'll jail him."

Weston was silent, his dark eyes on Price. They had a way of boring into a man as if probing every thought and feeling he had. Weston was at least sixty, but he looked younger. He had black hair that he wore long, and a spade beard equally black; these, with his erect posture, gave him an air of unbending dignity.

Pete Nance stood ten feet from Weston and a little behind him, his pale blue eyes showing faint amusement as they usually did. He was the only man Price had ever seen who carried two guns. His clothes were expensive but not gaudy. He was average height, average weight, average in every way, and therefore he puzzled Price completely. Without his guns, he was the kind of man who would never attract a second glance in a crowd, yet Price sensed he was a dangerous, cold-blooded killer.

Nance had been in the Elk River country about two months. Who he was and where he had come from were questions Price could not answer. He had never heard of the man before, so he was reasonably certain that Pete Nance was not his real name. The talk was that Weston had brought him here to kill Price, and Price believed the talk. It was a matter of when and how, but Price didn't think it would be now.

Irritated by Weston's contemptuous silence, Price said, "Get him to the doc, damn it."

"No hurry," Weston said. "You handle yourself pretty well, Regan."

"I've been here a year," Price said. "You should have known that before."

"I'd heard," Weston said, "but I hadn't seen you in action before." He paused, then added, "Carew has sent other deputies here who always got along. What's the matter with you?"

"Nothing," Price answered. "Always before Ralph let you pick your man, but some of the folks hereabouts thought it would be a good idea to have a deputy who wasn't your man."

Price saw interest sharpen the cattleman's expression. He asked, "Who?"

"Ralph didn't tell me."

Weston looked past Price at Blue, who hadn't stirred, then brought his gaze back to Price's face. "Regan, I've been a patient man, but I'm about done waiting. What are you going to do with Walt Cronin and that woman?"

"Nothing till I've got evidence against them," Price said. "I've already told Barry Madden." Then the anger that was close to the surface broke through. "You had it set up fine, didn't you? Real fine. Barry promises me a house so I can get married. I don't take it, so he tips you off and Curly jumps me. Then after I get bunged up, Nance is supposed to smoke me down." He wheeled to face the gunman. "Any time, Pete. I'm tired of waiting."

"Why, now," Nance said in his soft voice, "so am I, but the boss is kind of careful. We wait, but I don't know why. You'll have to ask him."

Without taking his eyes off Nance, Price said, "All right, Cole, I'm asking."

"Timing is the answer to a lot of problems," Weston said, "but maybe too much patience is a failing of mine.

I'm still hoping you'll take care of Cronin and the woman. If you do, you'll have no more trouble from me."

Slowly Price's gaze returned to Weston. He was sly and tricky and used to having his way, but he was careful just as Pete Nance had said. His men might fail as Curly Blue had failed, but Cole Weston never failed. That was how he had reached and kept the dominant position on Elk River that he held.

There was nothing to be gained by pushing now, Price thought. Through his bank, Madden controlled the townspeople, and Weston controlled Madden, but any control could be broken. This morning the townsmen had seen Weston's bully boy beaten into submission. So Weston could wait until the memory of Curly Blue lying here in the dust had faded a little in the minds of the townsmen.

"We'll see," Price said curtly, and walked past Weston into the livery stable.

As he was saddling his horse, Barney De Long came toward him along the runway. "You sure cooled Curly, Price," De Long said. "By golly, you done good."

Price tightened the cinch, then gave De Long a careful, studying look. He said, "Answer one question, Barney. Does the bank hold a note of yours? Or more than one?"

De Long backed away. "My business."

"It's mine, too. Every man on Main Street jumps whenever Madden whistles. Why, Barney? Is it because the bank could take your business away from you if you get out of line?"

Barney De Long wheeled and stalked away. Price stepped into the saddle and rode into the street. Weston and Nance had dragged Curly Blue to the trough and had sloshed water over his face until he had come around. Neither looked up as Price rode past.

As Price followed the road along the river to Cronin's store, he thought about what had happened since he'd been given the deputy's job in Saddle Rock nearly a year ago. Ralph Carew had known something about the situation here on Elk River, but only in a general way until he'd received the letters asking for a deputy who would not be Cole Weston's tool. Carew had never told Price how many letters he'd had, or who had written them, and that was just as well.

Carew, residing among the farm people around the county seat, had not suspected how bad conditions were on this side of the mountains even after he'd received the letters. But he had taken them seriously enough to recall the previous deputy and send Price, who had learned how things were the hard way, with the pressure gradually increasing on him through the months he had lived here. Now he would do what Barry Madden and the cowmen wanted him to do, or he'd run the risk of losing both his job and his girl.

He wondered whether Madden knew that Weston had planned to set Curly Blue on him, and Pete Nance with his gun after that. He couldn't be sure, but he didn't think so. Madden was a different breed of dog than Weston. At least he wanted to think so.

When Price had come here, he had not foreseen he would fall in love with Laura Madden, but he had. Right or wrong, it was a fact, and he couldn't change it. Now, as he considered his situation, he could think of no way out. He couldn't give Laura up, but, on the other hand, he sure as hell wasn't going to be told what to do by either Barry Madden or Cole Weston. He could only hope Laura would understand how it was.

Chapter 3

BELOW SADDLE ROCK THE ROAD PARALLELED ELK RIVER, AND
Price noticed that the water was high and roily and over
the banks in many places, lapping at the base of the
willows that ordinarily grew high above the edge of the
stream. Two weeks of hot, dry weather had brought
much of the snow out of the mountains, and it would not
be long before the pass was open. When it was, Price
would ride over the range and have a talk with Ralph
Carew.

The old sheriff had held his job for a generation. He
had been elected shortly after the Thornburg fight and
the Meeker massacre had given the politicians an excuse
to drive the Utes out of Colorado and open the western
slope for settlement. Within a few years he had tamed
the east half of Tremaine County while the west end was
still a wilderness, with Cole Weston and his Rocking C
crew the only inhabitants.

Carew was wise in the ways of men. He had often told
Price that outlaws were the least of a lawman's worries.
The real problems were wealthy men who, by intimida-
tion or bribery, used the law for their own ends. You

always had allies when you fought outlaws, but you went it alone against the man of property.

Well, he'd go it alone, Price thought bleakly. There was little to choose between Walt Cronin and the settlers on the Yellow Cat, and Madden and the cowmen. When a cowman like Cole Weston resorted to hiring gunmen of Pete Nance's caliber and bully boys like Curly Blue, Price was inclined to favor Cronin and the settlers, if a choice must be made.

His thoughts running sour, Price reined up and hipped around in the saddle to take a look at the mountains. He couldn't see them when he was in town because they were hidden by the foothills, so he often took this ride whether business brought him here or not.

He was unable to understand how people could live on the plains away from the mountains. As long as he could remember, he had received a strength and peace from them when he was troubled that he never found any-where else. This again was something he had never mentioned to Laura. She wouldn't understand it any more than she could understand his attitude about the star he carried.

Now, staring at the mountains, he was surprised how little snow was left up there in the high peaks, a dozen or more granite tips that made a long, gently curved set of sawteeth silhouetted against the blue sky. He could see the road, a thin, looping thread that reached above the ten-thousand-foot point before it made its final drive into a narrow canyon that led to the summit of Domino Pass.

The road, as far as he could follow it with his eyes, was clear of snow, but he knew that the trouble would be in canyons where the snow had piled up since the first storm last October. The stage to the county seat would not be running for another month, and it might be two or three weeks before even a horse could labor over the top.

He rode on, glancing at Cole Weston's Rocking C buildings across the river to the south. A sprawling stone house, big barns, corrals, sheds: all set on the slope above the river with hay meadows above and below the buildings.

Price had no idea how many head of cattle were under the Rocking C iron. He doubted if Weston knew. The rancher employed twenty or more men who were scattered among half a dozen subsidiary layouts on down the river and back among the rolling hills to the south. Besides these regular hands, he hired additional help during spring and fall roundups.

The range to the north belonged to the Mohawk boys' Broken Ring. Price had never been to the headquarters ranch, but he knew it was several miles from the river. On west of the Yellow Cat lay Red Sanders' Bridlebit. Both were smaller spreads than Weston's Rocking C. Still, they were big outfits, dwarfing the little ranches that clung to the tiny valleys in the foothills or lay far to the west in the arid badlands that stretched on to the Utah border and beyond.

All of this, Price thought, was an old and familiar pattern in the cattle country. The first man to reach a new range took what he wanted, and if, like Cole Weston, he was smart, greedy, and unscrupulous, he grew with the years. Then he was considered a natural leader by his neighbors because of his wealth, and the power that wealth gave him.

Weston was shrewd enough to include the Mohawks and Red Sanders in a sort of unofficial cattlemen's council. Barry Madden was part of it, too, because he had the bank, and a bank was an essential part of Weston's broad scheme of holding the Elk River country and keeping settlers out.

Price turned his thoughts to the possibility of a split between Madden and Weston, as he often did, but he had never been able to make up his mind how far Madden would go in backing the cowmen. If Price was able to promote a break, Weston could be whipped.

Price reached Cronin's store and tied at the hitch rack in front. The river made a steady rumble beyond the cottonwoods that lined the bank behind the store. On the other side of the road was Rose's cabin. No one denied what she was, and that included Cronin. The town of Saddle Rock wouldn't have put up with her for a minute, but out here no one could touch her, and even the settlers looked upon her as the epitome of evil and ignored her as much as they could.

The fact that Cronin had survived for better than a year was proof of his courage and fighting ability. He'd been shot at and hit twice; he'd shot back and killed at least one man. He was still here, a constant thorn in the side of the cowmen; but, judging from what had happened this morning, the end was near.

A tight fence behind Rose's cabin held a bunch of calves, all carrying Cronin's WC brand. Rose was no puzzle. She was a simple-minded woman who had found a place to ply her trade and was happy. But Cronin was a mystery. He was plainly a man who lived on hate and fire and fury, and sometimes he gave Price the impression he would actually welcome a fight with Cole Weston.

When Price entered the store, he found Rose sweeping behind the dry-goods counter. Cronin was on the opposite side, a cracker barrel on one hand, the end of a counter on the other. A shotgun lay across the cracker barrel within inches of his right hand. Cronin had seen him coming, Price thought, and was ready.

"Morning, Deputy," Cronin said belligerently.

"Howdy," Price said.

Rose leaned her broom against the counter and straightened up, her hands on her ample hips. She was not a good-looking woman. She was too plump, her features were rough, and she had oversized breasts that she showed off with stupid boldness by wearing low-cut dresses. Her brown hair was always frizzy, and quite often she gave the appearance of being not quite clean. To Price she was simply repulsive.

"You looking for me, Deputy?" Rose asked hopefully. "In a business way, I mean?"

"No. If I was looking for you, it wouldn't be in a business way."

Rose laughed. "Hell, man, nobody ever looks for me in any other way."

Ignoring her, Price turned his gaze to Cronin, who stared at him with pure hostility. Cronin said, "You ain't welcome here, Regan. You know that."

"So I've heard," Price said. "I've wondered why. Looks like you'd welcome the protection of the law."

Cronin snorted derisively. "Protection of the law, he says. Well, I can tell you mighty damned quick why you ain't welcome. You belong to Weston and the rest of them cow-nursing bastards."

"You're wrong," Price said. "I don't belong to anybody."

"You're a liar," Cronin shot back. "You wouldn't be wearing that star if you didn't belong to 'em."

Price rolled a cigarette, taking his time to answer. Cronin was a tall man with long legs and inordinately wide hips and narrow shoulders and a long neck. Oddly enough, his head was wide and square, resembling a box set on top of a post. He had red-flecked green eyes, a fat blob of a nose, and a meaty-lipped mouth.

A long scar, probably made by a knife, curled down the side of his face, giving the left end of his mouth a down twist. When he smiled, which was seldom, only the right side of his mouth curled upward. He was the ugliest man Price had ever seen, and one of the most vicious.

"You're still wrong," Price said finally. "I got the star from Ralph Carew in the county seat."

Cronin shrugged his shoulders. "Well, what do you want?"

"I'm curious about some things," Price said. "Looks like you've got a few more calves than you had the last time I was here."

"Go look at the brands if you figure I've been up to some funny business," Cronin challenged. "You won't find any of 'em worked over."

"No, you're too smart to work over a brand, but

there's a lot of talk about how you buy calves stolen from the ranches around here and brand them yourself."

"Got any proof?" Cronin demanded. "You've been smelling around here often enough. You ain't no fool, Regan. If there was any proof, you'd have found it."

Rose giggled. "How do you know he ain't a fool, Walt? He said he wasn't looking for me. I say that makes him a fool."

Price continued to ignore her. He said, "I never have savvied your setup, Cronin. Your business comes from the settlers up the Yellow Cat, but if they put all their money together they wouldn't have enough to buy a handkerchief to blow their nose. How do you get off?"

Cronin did grin then, his mouth curling up on one end and down on the other. "Regan, I don't give a damn how I come out as long as I get under Weston's hide. Reckon I have or you wouldn't be out here."

"You're under Madden's hide, anyhow," Price said. "This morning he told me to run you out of the country."

Cronin picked up his shotgun and pointed it at Price. "All right, Deputy. Start me to running."

"When and if I get the evidence I need," Price said, "I'll take you over the range to the county seat and you'll stand trial. That scattergun won't stop me, so don't count on it."

"Maybe I'll give you the evidence just to see if you can do the job," Cronin jeered. "I said you belonged to the cow nurses. Looks like this proves it."

Price shook his head. "No, it doesn't prove anything. I told you I'd arrest you when I had the evidence and no sooner. But it might be smart if you took Rose and sloped out of the country. I can't keep you from getting killed, Cronin. I figure something's about to blow or Madden wouldn't have talked to me the way he did."

He thought about telling Cronin that Weston had set Curly Blue on him and had planned for Pete Nance to finish it with his guns, and decided against it. Probably Cronin would only become more stubborn. He was certainly a man who wouldn't scare or he'd have been gone long ago.

Cronin stared at him, frankly inviting trouble. He said, "If they killed me'n Rose, you'd look the other way."

"No, I'll bring the man in who did it if I can find him," Price said. "Meanwhile you'll be dead, but I'm not going to worry about it. You're both parasites, and the country would be better off without you."

"I ain't no parasite," Rose screamed angrily. "I'm a respectable—"

"Oh, shut up!" Cronin said irritably. "Regan, you're looking out mostly for yourself, ain't you? Save you some trouble if we left the country, wouldn't it?"

"That's right."

"Well, we ain't leaving." Cronin jerked his head at the door. "Go on. Git."

Price walked out, knowing he had accomplished nothing. He hadn't even learned anything. Trouble was on the way if Cronin stayed. Price could smell it coming, the kind of trouble men would later be ashamed of.

The only way to avoid bloodshed was to arrest Cronin and get him out of the country. But that wasn't a permanent solution, either. Not as long as Cole Weston had the power he wielded now. Sooner or later there would be other Cronins, other settlers, and it would have to be done all over again. It was more than a matter of law. In the long run, the stake was a complete social and economic change for this entire section of Colorado, and only Cole Weston stood in the way. Once he was gone, the others could be handled.

Mounting, Price turned his roan up the Yellow Cat, convinced that tragedy was at hand, and he didn't know how to avert it. Then his thoughts turned back to what Barry Madden had said that morning. It would be his personal tragedy, too. If Laura was forced to choose between him and her father, he could not reasonably hope she would choose him.

Chapter 4

COLE WESTON WAS NOT FAMILIAR WITH FAILURE. IF HE HAD not been sure that Curly Blue could whip Regan, he would never have agreed to Blue's plan. Blue, who had been arrested and manhandled by Regan more times than he cared to remember, hated the deputy with a festering bitterness that he had never felt for anyone else, so the fight had been his idea to square accounts.

But Blue had failed. After he regained consciousness, he sat on the ground, his back against the water trough, a bruised and battered hulk of a man who lacked even the strength to recapture his hatred of the lawman who had beaten him.

Weston stared at Blue in loathing because he loathed all failures. After Price Regan rode by going downriver, Weston said to Pete Nance, "Get Curly on his horse and take him home."

"I didn't hire on to play nursemaid," Nance said in his mild tone.

Weston wheeled on him. "You'll do what I tell you or you'll draw your time." He swung around and strode to the bank, the edge of his fury blunted. He understood the pride that was in a man like Pete Nance and he didn't want to lose him. He didn't think he would, but he realized now it was a gamble he should never have taken.

When he went into the bank, John Ramey got down from his high stool. "Good morning, Mr. Weston," Ramey said in the obsequious tone he always used with him. "Go right on back. Mr. Madden is expecting you."

Weston swore and strode through the gate at the end of the counter and went on into Madden's office. It seemed to him there were just two kinds of people in the world: those who bowed and scraped in front of him because he was Cole Weston and those who defied him, men like Price Regan and Walt Cronin out there on the mouth of the Yellow Cat. He hated the latter and he despised the former.

Now, standing with his back to the door and glaring at Barry Madden, who glared back, Weston wasn't quite sure into which class he should put Madden. He wasn't quite sure, either, whether he could manage Madden if their relationship ever reached the breaking point. There were moments when the banker showed traces of a backbone. That bothered Weston. He needed Madden, needed him badly, but that was something Madden must never know.

"What did he say?" Weston demanded.

"You can guess," Madden said. "I offered to buy him the house. I told him it wouldn't be long before we had our own county and he'd be the first sheriff. He wanted to know what it would cost him, and I said all he had to do was to run Cronin out of the country. He got his neck bowed, so I said he'd lose both his job and his girl." Madden spread his hands. "Nothing worked. He said he'd handle Cronin when he got evidence against him."

Weston walked to the desk and helped himself to a cigar from the box in front of Madden, bit off the end and spat it in the general direction of the spittoon, then walked to the window and lighted it. He stared into the alley, thinking how much he could do with a man like Price Regan. The trouble was, you seldom found a man of his caliber, and when you did he was bound to be on the other side of the fence.

"We've waited too long, Barry," Weston said. "Now we've got to kill him."

He said it with as little emotion as if he had said he was going after a stock-killing bear. For a moment Barry Madden stared at his back, then said angrily, "You tried to kill Regan this morning. That wasn't in our agreement."

"No, it wasn't," Weston agreed. "You missed seeing a good fight, Barry. Regan could do pretty well in the prize ring. It's my guess he's had some training."

"I watched it from the bank." Madden rose and, putting his hands palm down against the desk, leaned forward. "Cole, I said that wasn't part of our agreement."

Weston turned, irritated by Madden's tone. "To hell with our agreement! You kept asking for time and I kept giving it to you on account of Laura. Regan's had plenty of chance. Now I'm done waiting. She'll find another man. She's young."

"We've got to try once more," Madden said. "I don't like Regan and he knows it, but that's not the point. If he's killed, Laura will hold it against me."

"She'll get over that, too," Weston said. "Sometimes you're a little stupid, Barry. There's more to this than just having a deputy we can't handle. There's more to it than letting Cronin steal a few calves and letting that bunch of sodbusters hang on."

"Stupid!" Madden said, getting red in the face. "If anyone's stupid, it's you for thinking you can go on forever making your own law."

Weston grinned. "No, I'm not stupid. I can't change. I've got to keep on. Cronin ain't hurting us and I don't need the Yellow Cat. Neither does Red Sanders or the Mohawk boys." He jabbed a forefinger at Madden. "The point is, sooner or later word will get out that them nesters have come here and they're staying. We'll get some land promoter in here and he'll advertise the country and the damned farmers will pour in by the hundreds. We're finished then, Barry. Our day's gone now. We're living on borrowed time and I aim to keep on borrowing time."

"I'm not finished," Madden said. "I'll still have a banking business."

Weston laughed at him. "The hell you will. But I'll tell you what you will have. You'll have competition, and you don't want that no more than I want farmers. We'll stay on top or we'll go down together. And if we do go down, you'll never get to the legislature."

Weston saw Madden's face turn pale; he watched him sit down at the desk again, suddenly, as if his knees had lost their strength and could not hold him any longer. Barry Madden had a dream that Weston had used time and time again to keep him in line, a dream so big and overpowering that it ruled everything Madden did. The only rival it had was Laura, and now, watching Madden, Weston sensed the old struggle that had gone on in Madden from the time his wife had died and Laura had become doubly important to him.

Sweat made a bright shine on Madden's forehead. He took a white handkerchief out of his pocket and wiped his face. Then he said, "I know you're right about what'll happen once we get a real flood of farmers coming over the pass, but twelve hours won't change anything. Give me that much time, Cole. For Laura."

"You still think Regan will change, after the way you put it up to him this morning?" Weston shook his head. "You're crazy, Barry."

"I've got to make one more try. Red Sanders and the Mohawk boys will be in town this afternoon, today being Saturday. So far I've been the one to talk to Regan. Maybe I went at it wrong, trying to buy him with a house. Well, I want all of you to be at my place this evening and we'll make it plain. I'll have Max Harker there, too, so Regan will think the townsmen are behind us."

Weston gave this a moment's thought. Then he said, "No, twelve hours won't make any difference. You won't change Regan, but you can try, if you'll go along with us after he turns you down."

"With you? I mean, what are you planning?"

"I don't know yet. I just want your word you'll back us."

Reluctantly Madden nodded. "All right, you've got it."

"If you break it, I'll kill you, Barry. Don't ever doubt it."

Weston walked to the door and put his hand on the knob, then looked back at Madden, his dark eyes faintly speculating. No real guts in the man, he thought. He belonged to the bowing and scraping class, and the funny part of it was he didn't need to be because the truth was that Weston needed Madden a hell of a lot more than Madden needed Weston.

"I'll kill you, Barry," Weston said again. "Remember that."

He went out, shutting the door behind him, pleased by this arrangement. Regan could be put out of the way any time. Now he had Barry Madden exactly where he wanted him. Red Sanders and the Mohawks would be easy to handle. So would the storekeeper, Max Harker.

He crossed the street to the livery stable and got his horse, Barney De Long treating him in the same obsequious manner that John Ramey had. He rode out of town slowly, thinking ahead to what must be done after what would be a fruitless and perhaps unpleasant session with Regan.

Damn a man like that, anyhow, and damn Ralph Carew for sending him here. That brought his thoughts to the letters Ralph Carew had received. He wondered who had sent them. He'd find out, someway, and he'd deal with him when the time came. Or them. He had no idea how many people had written to Carew.

He rode slowly, making his plans as he rode. He glanced at the rolling hills north of the river, Broken Ring range that belonged to the Mohawks. He found satisfaction in the thought that they were here on Elk River only because he permitted it. He had let them stay because he could use them, tough, ruthless men who would not hesitate at a killing any more than he would. Red Sanders on the other side of the Yellow Cat was weak, but he'd go along because he had no choice. He had a young wife and small children. That was good, adding something that he and the Mohawks lacked.

With Barry Madden, he had everything. No need to worry about the changing times. He'd make time hold still here on Elk River for as long as he lived, and he sure didn't give a damn about anything that happened afterward.

Suddenly his thoughts went sour. He was only fooling himself, and what was the sense in that? He had gone a long ways, coming here in the days when the Elk River country belonged to the Utes, and he had no business on this side of the mountains.

He had stayed because he knew how to handle the Indians. He had fed them in his kitchen. He had given them beef when they were hungry and when the government supplies had failed to come in from Rawlins. He knew the chiefs: Douglas, Captain Jack, Colorow, Piah, Johnson, and even some like Ouray and Shavano who remained along the Uncompahgre to the south.

When the Meeker and Thornburg trouble had come, he'd been successful in walking the tightrope and had kept out of trouble. Even after the Utes had been sent to Utah and marauding bands had come back across the border, he still had been let alone because the Indians remembered he had been their friend.

Through these years he had ruled the Elk River country by one method or another, even murdering when necessary, and he had kept the settlers out of the fertile land along the river. He had waited for the Mohawks and Sanders to take care of Walt Cronin and the nesters on the Yellow Cat, but they hadn't done anything, though he had been after them long enough to do it. He'd waited, and waiting wasn't his way. Maybe he was getting a little soft with age. Well, he was done waiting now. Twelve hours. No more.

Turning off the road, he crossed the bridge and followed the lane to the headquarters ranch, fine buildings, the best in the country. He tried to admire them as he had in the past; he tried to think of his wealth, cattle and horses and cash in Barry Madden's bank, but somehow there was no real satisfaction in anything today.

He asked himself what he really had, what he would leave when he died, and he swore aloud. By God, nothing. A wife who had never given him a child, a wife who had been scared of her own shadow from the day they were married. Satisfactions that were part of the daily life of a man like Red Sanders, who would never amount to anything, had been denied him.

He put his horse into a run, digging him hard with his spurs. He reined up in front of the corral gate in a cloud of dust and turned the animal over to his choreman. As he strode toward the house, Pete Nance appeared from the bunkhouse.

"Curly lit out," he said. "Didn't say where he was going, but he was sure madder'n hell."

Weston stared at the gunman, hating him as he hated everything and everybody at this moment. He said, "I've held back on Regan because of Madden, but it won't be much longer."

"Good," Nance said. "I'm getting tired of this country."

Weston went on, thinking he'd feel better if he told Nance he was tired of having him around, but there was no sense in that. Nance had come at a high price and he hadn't started to earn his wages yet.

Weston went across the dusty yard into the house,

slamming the door behind him, and looked around at the fine mahogany furniture and the high-piled Brussels carpet and the red silk drapes at the windows. There had been a time when his social ambitions had run high and he had put out good money for these things, and not once had his wife entertained anybody unless he had nagged for weeks, and then she made a poor show of it.

"Lily!" he bellowed. "Where the hell are you, Lily?"

She came running out of the kitchen, wiping her wet hands on her apron. "What is it, Cole?"

She never looked at him. She always looked past or over him or at the floor in front of him. "Dinner ready?" he demanded.

"No. It isn't noon yet. I didn't know when you'd be here, Cole."

"Get it!" he shouted. "God damn it, get it!"

"Yes, Cole," she said, and ran back into the kitchen.

He dropped down into a leather-covered chair, feeling empty and a little sick and washed out. Sixty years old and here he was, with nothing. He should have divorced Lily years ago and married a woman who could have children. He could even have adopted a boy. But it was too late, too late for anything.

He thought of Price Regan, then of Walt Cronin and the lice on the Yellow Cat who called themselves farmers. They wouldn't be there much longer, he told himself. They'd been there far too long now.

Suddenly the emptiness was gone from him and he was filled with a strange, quiet fury that fastened on Walt Cronin because Cronin was responsible for the settlers staying, and so Cronin represented everything that Weston hated.

Not Regan, because Regan was a man he could respect, but no one respected Walt Cronin. He'd hang the bastard, and every settler on the Yellow Cat would be out of the country by sundown. He felt better now that he thought about it. Hanging Cronin would settle everything.

Chapter 5

THE YELLOW CAT WAS A SMALL STREAM THAT HEADED AMONG the low sage-covered hills to the north. Its valley was narrow and barren in most places, a sort of No Man's Land between Broken Ring and Bridlebit that no one wanted. That was the reason, Price thought as he rode up the creek after leaving Cronin's store, that Cronin and the settlers had been permitted to stay.

If the Yellow Cat had been south of the river on Weston's Rocking C range, the nesters would have been moved the day they arrived, but being north of the river, they had been out of Weston's immediate reach, and neither Sanders nor the Mohawks had taken the trouble to evict them.

For weeks Weston had been saying in town that he was losing calves and that Walt Cronin was responsible. It could be true, Price thought, but the small number of calves that were stolen wasn't a drop in the bucket to Cronin's neighbors. Certainly Red Sanders figured it didn't amount to enough to kick up a fuss over, and the Mohawk brothers didn't have time. They were too niggardly to hire the men they needed, so they had to work twice as hard as they would otherwise have done.

Sooner or later Price's thinking always got around to Cole Weston, and he asked himself why Weston was making an issue about the settlers' presence when his grass was not endangered. It could be that the rancher was using the settlers as an excuse to get rid of a deputy he couldn't handle. That could be part of the answer, Price decided, but it seemed more likely to be a simple matter of principle. Weston hated settlers whether they were on his range or not. He had a one-track mind that, once settled upon a course of action, would never detour or stop until the job was done or he was dead. A big question in Price's mind was why Weston had waited as long as he had to get Cronin out of the country.

As far as the valley of the Yellow Cat was concerned, it was a poverty range that wasn't worth fighting about. The creek faded to a trickle during dry seasons, and sometimes the nesters had to go to the river to fill their barrels with water. A few had wells, most of them didn't, and occasionally even the wells went dry.

In places the walls flanking the Yellow Cat rose a sheer hundred feet, the canyon narrowing so there was barely room for a wagon to go between the creek on one side and the cliff on the other. Every half-mile or so the canyon widened out into a pocket where there were fifty or sixty acres of flat land. In all of these pockets settlers had built houses, usually tarpaper shacks, and were trying to eke out a living.

Price knew these people. They were, with one or two exceptions, a pretty scurvy lot, men who had drifted all over the West with their wives and kids and rickety wagons and worn-out teams, wanderers who had consistently failed at everything they'd tried and would have failed here if Walt Cronin hadn't kept them from starving to death.

The creek was choked with brush the entire length of the valley. By the time Price reached Frank Evans's place, he'd seen a dozen or more WC yearlings in the brush. Probably there were others he hadn't seen. As Price reined off the road and pulled up beside the garden Evans was hoeing, he wondered if Cronin was carrying on a bigger operation than he suspected.

Evans was a bachelor, a stooped, middle-aged man who had a hungry look about him just as the rest of the settlers did. Now he stopped and leaned on his hoe, staring at Price truculently.

"Morning, Frank," Price said.

"Howdy," Evans grunted, giving no invitation to Price to step down.

"How's your garden coming?" Price asked.

"Poorly."

The rocky ground was dry and hard, and the vegetables did indeed look poorly. There was no evidence that Evans had tried to irrigate, although the creek was bank full and it would have been an easy task to run a ditch around the edge of the meadow so that the garden and the field of sickly looking oats could have been watered as long as the stream ran as high as it was now.

Evans continued to lean on his hoe, letting Price feel the edge of his hostility. Although he'd never had any trouble with the settlers, Price knew they hated him simply because Cronin had poisoned them against him, convincing them he was Weston's man.

"How many yearlings do you suppose Cronin owns?" Price asked. Evans licked his lips, gaze dropping away from Price. "Dunno."

"How many cows does he own?"

"Dunno."

"Kind of funny, isn't it?"

"What's funny?"

"Cronin's got a bunch of calves in his pasture and I've seen some yearlings along the creek, but I haven't spotted any cows."

Evans started to hoe, saying nothing. Price turned his horse back to the road and went on up the creek. He was wasting his time. These people wouldn't say anything against Cronin whether they were doing the stealing or not.

But Price had to make them talk. Once the shooting started, there'd be hell to pay, with as many women and kids strung out along the creek as there were. Buildings would be burned, the people who resisted would be killed, and the rest would be scared half to death and lose the meager possessions they did have.

Price had seen this kind of thing happen. It had to be stopped before it started. There was a slim chance some of these people might say the wrong thing. If he could dig up any evidence against Cronin, he'd hustle the man out of the country and for the time being the trouble would be averted.

Sam Potter lived just above Evans with his wife, his daughter Jean, and a boy named Bruce Jarvis who worked for his room and board. The Potter place was the best-looking farm on the creek. They owned a saddle horse as well as a good team; the house was painted; the garden and grain looked good; and there was no manure pile back of the barn. As far as Price knew, Potter was the only farmer on the creek who had enough gumption to scatter his manure on his garden and fields.

Potter was tinkering around his wagon when Price rode up. An instant later Mrs. Potter came from the house and the girl Jean left the henhouse, both moving across the yard to stand together a few feet behind Potter.

Price said, "Good morning."

Potter tipped his head in greeting, saying nothing. Neither did his wife. The boy Bruce slipped around the barn and stood watching. Absolute silence for a minute, all four of them showing the same hostility that had been in Frank Evans.

The Potters were a notch above the rest of the creek people, and now it struck Price that if he couldn't get through to them he might just as well ride back to town.

There'd be no point in going on up the creek.

Anger stirred in Price as his gaze moved from Potter's round face to his wife's thin, sharp one, and on to Jean, who was about twenty and who would be attractive if she had some decent clothes to wear. He had never seen her in anything but a faded and patched gingham dress similar to the one she was wearing now.

He glanced at Bruce, a skinny kid of sixteen or seventeen, with a hint of peach fuzz on his chin and upper lip and hands that were oddly big for so thin a boy. His clothes, which were too large for him, consisted mostly of patches sewed on patches, probably Sam Potter's castoffs that had been worn out when he'd given them to Bruce.

"Well, you folks are sure a friendly bunch," Price burst out.

"Why should we be friendly?" Mrs. Potter demanded. "That star you're packing don't mean nothing. You're a hired gun who sold your soul to Cole Weston and now you're here to tell us to leave the country. Ain't that right?"

"You're wrong, ma'am," Price said. "This star does mean something. I'm not a hired gun, and I haven't sold my soul to Cole Weston."

"But you did come to tell us to leave the country, didn't you?" Mrs. Potter pressed.

He didn't answer for a moment, his gaze returning to Jean. He thought again she was good looking, with her chestnut hair and dark blue eyes that were well spaced. A trim figure, too, inside the faded dress that fitted her like a wool sack. Even her toes poked through the front of her shoes.

Poverty, he thought bitterly, the kind of terrible, shameful poverty that should never exist in a country as wealthy as this, and yet the Potters were better off than anyone else on the creek.

"Sam," Price said, his eyes returning to Potter, "what have you got here that's worth staying for?"

"A home," Mrs. Potter answered for her husband. "We've been here longer than any other place since we got married. We ain't moving again, Regan. That's a promise."

Price kept his gaze on Potter, ignoring his wife. He felt ashamed and sorry for a man who'd let a hatchet-faced wife do his talking for him. He asked softly, "Don't you have a tongue, Sam?"

Potter grinned placidly. "I got one, but I don't use it much. Lizzie, she talks better'n I do."

"And I'm going to talk some more," Mrs. Potter said in her strident voice. "We ain't hurting nobody, the Mohawks or Sanders or Weston or nobody. We just want to be let alone. We're going to prove up on this place. No reason we should be pushed off of it. If they kill us, our blood's going to soak into this land. We're never moving, mister. Get that through your thick head."

"Ma," Jean said. "You don't have to insult him."

"Insult a gunslinger like him?" Mrs. Potter reared back so that her thin, droopy breasts made twin lumps under her dress, her gaunt cheeks turning dark red. "Jean, you don't understand men like this. They're killers. They're paid to run over weak people like us. Chase us off land that nobody wants just because we ain't rich with cattle like Cole Weston."

"You're wrong again, ma'am," Price said. "I aim to see you have the right to live on this place if you don't break any laws. That's why I'm here. Looks to me like Walt Cronin's been stealing calves, but I haven't found the evidence I need to arrest him. When I do, he'll go to the county seat for trial, but right now there's one thing you folks ought to think about. How will you make out when he's gone?"

"We'll make out," Mrs. Potter said bitterly. "Don't you ever think we won't, but I reckon you won't arrest Cronin. He's smarter'n you are."

"Then he has been stealing calves?"

"I didn't say that."

"If he isn't, who is? Are you folks doing it for him, or is it some of the cowboys who come to see Rose?"

"I don't know nothing about it," Mrs. Potter said through tight lips. "Neither does Sam. You go on now. Just leave us alone."

Price glanced at the boy, who was staring at him, his eyes pinned on the gun holstered on Price's thigh, then at Jean, who was trying to smile, trying to tell him they didn't really hate him the way her mother was making out.

"I feel sorry for you folks because you're stupid," Price said. "There's places where you could live on good land with good water rights, but you've got to come here where you'll never make a living, and you're backing up a crook who's just about got to the end of his twine."

Price reined around and rode back downstream, Mrs. Potter yelling at his back, "Don't feel sorry for us, coming around here and trying to scare us with that kind of talk when you ain't fit to breathe the same air . . ."

"Ma," Jean cried. "Stop it!"

"He's right, Lizzie," Sam Potter said. "He's more right than you can see."

More talk, loud and angry, but Price didn't go back. Or even look back. No use. Nothing could change Lizzie Potter. She was stubborn and mean, but maybe it was a meanness that had been forced upon her by a hard life. Maybe she was so tired of drifting from one place to another that she'd rather die here than start drifting again.

Then he thought of Jean and shook his head. In another twenty years she might be like her mother, but she wasn't now. She deserved a better life than she had here on the Yellow Cat, a better future.

Who was to blame? Her mother? Walt Cronin? Or was it Cole Weston and Barry Madden and the rest who had closed off the good land along Elk River?

No, it was bigger than that, Price thought. It was the Westons and the Maddens all over the West who had kept the Potters drifting from one place to another, and even now would not let them rest on the Yellow Cat. The lawmen, too, men like himself. And Ralph Carew. That, he decided grimly, would in the end be the real issue here. Either men had a right to settle on the public domain, or you forgot your oath to enforce the law; you traded your integrity for the right to live.

If Price had learned anything from Ralph Carew, it was the conviction that a man who traded his integrity had no right to live. But could he make Laura understand that?

Chapter 6

PRICE HAD LITTLE RESPECT FOR PEOPLE WHO MOVED FROM ONE failure to another. He had less respect for men like Walt Cronin, who used weaker people for his selfish gain, and women like Rose who lived without feeling the limitations of moral precepts.

But they were the outcasts, the have-nots. In a way they were pathetic, hanging by their fingernails to the edge of a society that should have allowed them a better life. Therein, Price thought as he rode down the Yellow Cat, lay the real trouble. He knew that justice was never absolute; it did not depend strictly upon the word of the law, but must be diluted with mercy, a much needed and seldom used commodity.

To all intents and purposes, the Homestead Act had been repealed on Elk River. Cole Weston—and he was a common type in a raw country like this—considered any law a tool to be used for his personal profit, to be overlooked when it could not be used.

But now, in spite of his personal feelings and in spite of what had happened this morning, Price was being forced to the cowmen's side. He had to get Cronin because Cronin was the only one so far who had committed overt acts against the law. There was still the matter of securing evidence against him, but sooner or later he'd make a mistake and Price would have what he needed.

Once that Walt Cronin was gone from Elk River, the problem would be solved—a wrong solution, but it would be solved. The settlers would be starved into leaving the Yellow Cat, and the cowmen would have what they wanted. Otherwise the settlers would be destroyed. Moving them out was the best thing that could happen to them, but they would never agree to that. They would hate him even more than they did now.

Price Regan stood alone, as terribly alone as a man could be, but that was the cost of being a lawman. Ralph Carew had often told him that, told him how he, too, had stood alone in the early days on the other side of the Singing Wind Range.

Price had listened, but he had not really understood because it hadn't happened to him. He understood now, and he thought of Laura. He should have known, he told himself bitterly, months ago, before he asked her to marry him. Now it was too late, and she would be hurt before it was over.

He rode past Frank Evans's place. The farmer was still in his garden, not even bothering to look up as Price went by. A few minutes later he reached Cronin's store. The man must have been watching for him. Now he stepped off the porch and into the road, calling, "Regan."

Price reined up. "Well?"

"What have you been up to?"

"Looking," Price answered. "You know what I saw?"

"I don't give a damn what you saw."

"I figure you'd better. Calves here in your pasture, Cronin. Yearling steers up the creek, but no cows. Where did you get them?"

"My business," Cronin said sullenly.

"Yesterday I might have agreed," Price said, "but not

today. A lot of people live up that creek. Some of them are going to get hurt. I aim to keep it from happening if I can."

Cronin wasn't wearing his gun. Now he reared back, hands shoved under his waistband, eyes on Price as if seeing him in a new light. "What are you aiming to do, Deputy?"

"I've asked a few questions," Price said. "I'm going to keep on asking till I find out where those calves came from. I think you stole them. Or somebody stole them for you. You must have had help branding them. Frank Evans, probably, since he's the closest."

"You figure you can get a conviction on what you think?" Cronin demanded.

"No. If I thought so, you'd have been arrested before this. You're a tough nut, Walt, but the boys up the Yellow Cat aren't. I'll arrest Evans on suspicion of rustling. Give him a few days in jail and he'll talk. If he don't, Sam Potter will when I get him away from his wife. I'll get a sworn statement out of one of them, and that'll be enough to send you to Canon City for twenty years."

Cronin blew out a great breath and cursed. He said, "Get down off that horse, Regan. I'm going to beat you to death."

"I don't figure to give you a chance," Price said, and reached for his gun.

"Get down," Rose said.

She was standing in front of her cabin, a cocked shotgun in her hands. So this was the way they had set it up. He saw it with stark clarity. A bullet, a drowning in the river, even an accident up the Yellow Cat: anything of the sort would have pointed suspicion at Cronin. But if Price took a beating that put him in bed for weeks, or if he were permanently maimed so he had to quit his job, Walt Cronin would be no worse off than he was right now. People would say it was too bad the deputy wasn't made of tougher stuff.

He had no choice. Rose had an ugly look on her face as

if she would just as soon pull the trigger as not. Cronin said, "Better do what she says, Regan. I don't want to see you shot, but she'll do it if you make her."

"Either way I lose," Price said. "If I whip you, she'll shoot me."

Cronin laughed. "You won't whip me, bucko, but if you do you ride out, providing you can get on a horse."

Price glanced at Rose again. She said, "Hurry up, damn it. Get your butt out of that saddle."

Price stepped down, wondering if he had any chance if he pulled his gun. But Cronin was unarmed, and shooting a woman even under these circumstances went against his grain. But these were foolish scruples. The plain truth was that if he made a move for his holstered gun, Rose would blow him apart with buckshot.

"Take off your gun belt," Cronin said. "Hang it over the saddle horn. Then tie your horse." He motioned to the hitch rack in front of the store.

Price obeyed and stepped away from his horse. Then Cronin was on him, swinging a great fist up from his knees, and Rose shrieked, "Kill him, Walt! Kill the bastard!"

Price tipped his head to one side, Cronin's fist ripping his ear. He caught Cronin with an upswinging right that jarred him but didn't stop him. The man was bigger than Price, and stronger; he was like a bull with a single idea in his head. He kept boring in, striking with his left and then his right.

Backing up, Price took the blows on his shoulders as much as he could, or on his arms. He knew it wasn't any good. He couldn't win a fight by blocking the other man's punches, and when he did connect, his blows seemed to have no more effect on Cronin than a gnat buzzing in his ear.

The trouble was, he couldn't land a solid punch. He was always off balance, ducking and feinting and pivoting in a desperate effort to keep from being knocked out by one of Cronin's roundhouse blows. It would have taken only one, for Cronin's fists carried the authority of a mule kick.

Price circled to keep from being pinned against the wall of Rose's cabin. Like a blood-lusting school kid watching a recess fight, Rose kept screaming, "Kill him, Walt! Kill the bastard!" She must have run out of breath, for suddenly she was silent, and there was no sound except the roar of the river and their labored breathing and the whisper of boots in the dust.

The pattern of the fight was set. Price steadily retreating and circling so that now they had returned to the place where they had started. Like Curly Blue earlier today, Cronin was not an imaginative man. He didn't vary the pattern; he seemed satisfied to keep pursuing Price, to keep throwing punches, confident that sooner or later he'd nail Price on the jaw and that would end it. He did get a blow through that was partially blocked, but still had enough steam behind it to jar Price and hurt him, and for a moment Cronin's face was a blur.

Now his retreat was a headlong rout. He had to keep out of Cronin's way until his head cleared. If he stumbled and fell, he was finished, for Cronin would give him his boot and he'd be lucky if he wasn't killed.

That one blow verified what he already knew, that he had to change tactics. He did, suddenly and without warning. He waited until Cronin was slightly off balance, having missed one of his tremendous uppercuts; then Price reversed himself and, bending low, charged headlong into Cronin, his head hitting the man in the belly.

Price heard wind go out of Cronin, a long *ooof,* and for a short moment Cronin seemed paralyzed as his empty lungs searched for breath. His mouth was open, his eyes distended. Price brought his head up in a savage thrust. He caught Cronin square under the chin; he heard teeth snap together, and as he stepped back he saw blood run down Cronin's chin. He'd bitten his lip or his tongue.

Price swarmed all over him, hitting him hard and fast with both fists. He nailed Cronin on the temple, on the opposite side of the head, on the nose and on the chin. Cronin floundered, badly hurt, fists clubbing at Price but doing no great damage. Then Price had the opening he wanted. He sledged Cronin with a straight right to the jaw, and Cronin's legs went rubbery and he fell.

Price dropped on him, knees driving savagely into the man's belly, and he hit him on the face, rocking his head to one side and then the other. Rose screamed, "Get off!" and prodded him in the back with the muzzle of her shotgun. "Get off him, damn you!"

Cronin wasn't knocked cold, but as Price got to his feet and backed away Cronin showed no inclination to get up. Rose kept the shotgun pointed at Price. She was crying, tears running down her face. "Get up, Walt." She wiped a dirty sleeve across her face. "You can whip him, Walt. Get up."

Cronin raised himself on one elbow and fell back. Blood ran down his face from his nose and his mouth and made red streaks on his chin and neck. He said through bruised lips, "I'm licked."

"Want me to shoot his God-damned head off?" Rose demanded. "I can do it."

She could, all right, Price thought, still backing up and turning toward his horse, and for a horrible moment he thought she would before Cronin said, "No, let him go."

Price reached his roan. He untied the reins and pulled himself into the saddle and rode away, still half expecting a load of buckshot in his back. But none came, and presently he was out of range.

When he thought it was safe, he turned to the riverbank and, dismounting, knelt and sloshed water over his face and arms and shoulders. He stood up, dizzy for a moment, feeling the beating he had taken. His face hadn't been marked except for a bruise under one eye and a cut on his right cheek, but his forearms and shoulders seemed to be one great solid ache.

He mounted and rode back to town. He'd been lucky, and he had to give grudging admission that Cronin, lying in the dust and badly beaten, had saved his life. One word from him and Rose would have pulled the trigger.

He put his horse away and stepped into the street. Max Harker, the storekeeper, was waiting for him. He asked, "Have a little trouble?"

"I've been up Yellow Cat," Price said. "Caught some brush in the face."

Harker gave him his cynical grin. He said, "Like hell." Price would have gone on if Harker hadn't gripped his arm. "I want to talk to you. I saw you ride into town and came over."

Price backed up to the front wall of the stable and leaned against it. Harker was a queer one. In the months that Price had been in Saddle Rock, he hadn't got acquainted with the man. At times he wondered if anyone knew Harker. He had come here ten years ago, so the story ran, a lunger who expected to die and claimed he was still waiting to die. He was a slender man who coughed often, his face pale except for the two spots of red on his cheeks.

"All right," Price said. "Talk."

"You've got trouble," Harker said. "Barry Madden came to me this morning and asked me to take the marshal's badge."

That was like Madden. He moved fast, too fast. He had no power to hire or fire a town marshal, but the council would probably back him up. Price said, "Looks like I'm out of a job."

"Not till night," Harker said. "Maybe not till Monday. You've still got a chance if you go see Barry and sing the right song. He'll furnish you with the words. All you need is the tune."

"He can go to hell."

Harker shrugged his skinny shoulders. "I thought you'd say that. Kind of a joke, asking me to be marshal. I'm a fair hand with a gun, but going into a saloon and fetching out drunk cowboys and throwing them into jail is out of my line."

"They don't want that," Price said. "That's one thing I've done that got Weston down on me."

"I know," Harker said. "So I'm a good choice. Still funny, I say. I should have died ten years ago, but consumption didn't get me. Now a dose of hot lead will. Well, who cares? I'm one man in this town who can die without anybody shedding one damned tear. That's the kind of man they want, Price."

"They're wrong, Max. Wrong in the way they think and act. A lot of people are going to get hurt if Cole Weston doesn't get cut down a notch."

"Then crawl," Harker said. "Crawl to Barry Madden so he'll let you keep the star. You're the only man in this end of the county who can handle this job."

"No, I won't crawl," Price said. "Not for Barry Madden or any man."

He walked away. He had to get a shave and haircut and a bath. He had a date with Laura for the dance tonight, and he wondered what Barry Madden would say when he rang the doorbell.

Chapter 7

BRUCE JARVIS HAD NOT KNOWN ANY REAL SECURITY FROM THE time his parents had died of scarlet fever when he was ten and the Potters had taken him. He hadn't been in school a day since then; he had very seldom had the satisfaction of having his stomach full; he had not known love except from Jean Potter, who was all a sister could have been to him.

The only other bright spot in Bruce's life was the younger Farnum girl Susie. The Farnums had the next place on the Yellow Cat above Potter's. Lizzie Potter was always talking about what a shiftless lot they were, with George Farnum stealing a calf for Walt Cronin whenever he got a chance, or butchering a steer and selling the beef to Cronin. Then there was the older girl Dora, who sneaked up to the rim and carried on with a Bridlebit or Broken Ring cowboy whenever she had a chance.

But Susie wasn't like Dora. She was sixteen, just a few months younger than Bruce. She always wanted to hold Bruce's hand whenever she had a chance, and if she could get him away from the others she liked to be kissed.

It was exciting to kiss her, but kind of scary, too. She wanted to get married, but he knew he was a long ways from being ready for that. He needed to talk to someone about it, but there wasn't anybody. Not even Jean. She still thought he was a kid and she'd just laugh. Maybe she'd tell her mother, and then there'd be hell to pay. He was scared of Lizzie's long tongue more than anything else in the world. It seemed to grow sharper with the years, and it ought to, the way she honed it on him every day.

He hated Lizzie, and he had nothing but contempt for Sam because Sam let his wife run him. He never stood up to her. He never made a decision. She did all the talking just as she had today when that deputy Price Regan was here. Sam just grunted, or smiled blandly, and kept still.

But Jean was made of different stuff. For a long time she fought with her mother. Finally she had enough of it. Just a few weeks ago she'd said: "You're not going to talk to me any more like that. I'm twenty years old. I can get a man if I have to. Or I can go to Saddle Rock and get a job. I will, too, if you don't hush up."

Lizzie had hushed up, all right, but that only made it worse on Sam and Bruce. She'd always squeezed every bit of work out of Bruce she could, and now she was on him if he took a long breath. As soon as the deputy rode off, she said to Bruce: "You get over on that woodpile. We ain't got enough wood for supper. You hear now?"

He heard and obeyed, rebellion growing in him until he knew he couldn't stand it any longer. He'd run away. There was going to be trouble here and he didn't want any part of it. They were all fools, Frank Evans and Sam Potter and George Farnum and the rest of them up the Yellow Cat, sucking around after Walt Cronin and stealing calves for him and getting deeper into debt all the time.

He pulled on the crosscut until he was out of breath. Every time he stopped to wipe the sweat off his face, he expected to hear Lizzie yell at him from the back door.

As soon as a cut cropped off the log, he picked up the ax and split it, then he started on the log again. All the time he was thinking about what he'd do.

He'd talk to Susie this evening. The settlers gathered at Cronin's store every Saturday night. The men drank all their credit would stand, and the women bought a little of this or that, but mostly it was a social occasion.

The settlers had little to do but gossip. They took care of some of it on Saturday nights, and picked it up again on Sunday mornings when they gathered at the Potter place. They always had a service of sorts, with Sam preaching a sermon that Lizzie wrote for him during the week. She'd have preached it herself if the Bible hadn't strictly said women couldn't speak up in church.

After the service there was always potluck dinner, with the women gabbling like a bunch of geese and the kids running around, the boys chasing the girls and the girls squealing. Sooner or later one of the boys would stumble and fall and wind up with his face in a dish of beans, then he'd get a whopping and he'd run off bawling for all he was worth. About that time Bruce would sneak off with Susie.

The more he thought about running away, the more he knew he was in a bind. He couldn't do anything if he was on foot. He had to have a horse to get a job, but he couldn't buy one. He didn't have five cents to his name. All he ever got from the Potters were his meals and a place to sleep and hand-me-down clothes that were too big for him.

Well, he'd steal Potter's saddle horse. He had that much coming and more. But Lizzie wouldn't see it that way. She'd get the deputy Regan after him, and they'd hang him if they caught him, but he'd make sure he didn't get caught.

Lizzie called him to supper and he carried an armload of wood into the house and dropped it into the box behind the stove. Lizzie talked all through the meal just as she always did. Sometimes she got so far behind in her eating that she had to finish after the rest were done and had left the table.

"You go harness up," she told Bruce. "I want to get to the store ahead of everybody else."

She always tried, and sometimes she succeeded. Not that she ever actually bought anything. There wasn't anything new to see, either, for Cronin hadn't been able to get over Domino Pass to the county seat since last fall, and he wouldn't, or couldn't, buy anything in Saddle Rock. Max Harker refused to sell to him except at regular retail prices, and Cronin wouldn't pay them.

But it didn't make any difference to Lizzie whether there was anything new to see or not. She loved to stand at the dry-goods counter and look enviously at the hats, or feel the cloth on a bolt, or stare at the corsets and whisper to Jean that they were lucky they didn't have to cinch themselves like most women so they couldn't breathe.

Bruce guessed it was the same with Lizzie as it was with him. He used to stand for an hour at a time in front of the candy counter and stare at the gumdrops and jelly beans and licorice and peppermint while his mouth watered so much he had to keep swallowing. Now it was the gun rack instead of the candy counter.

Tonight Bruce had to grease the wagon, and for no reason except perverseness he took his time. He dawdled harnessing the team and he was slow hooking up, and all of Lizzie's nagging didn't hurry him. She wasn't any more successful with Sam, who shaved in the kitchen, and Jean, who was the last one to get dressed. By the time they were in the wagon, they heard the Farnum rig coming down the creek and Sam allowed they might just as well wait for their neighbors.

Lizzie was so worn out with an hour of straight-hand fretting that she couldn't talk. She sat on the seat beside Sam, straight-backed, her bony hands laced on her lap, her face sour enough to clabber milk. Bruce liked to tell Susie that Lizzie could make smearcase out of milk sooner than anyone else on the Yellow Cat. All she had to do was stand and stare at a pan of fresh milk for five minutes and it turned to clabber.

When the Farnum rig pulled up beside the Potter wagon, George Farnum sang out, "Butchered me a Broken Ring steer today. I was up on the rim this morning and spotted this critter, so I choused him down Morning Glory gulch and slaughtered him. I taken me a hindquarter and I've got the rest here for Cronin. You want a quarter, Sam?"

"No," Lizzie said. "The deputy was out here today smelling around. You keep that stealing up, George Farnum, and they'll clap you into jail."

Farnum was a big, bald-headed man who had lost his wife the year before. He didn't seem to give a damn about anything, not even what his girl Dora did when she sneaked off to the rim to be with a cowboy, or what Susie and Bruce did when they were alone in the brush. At least that was what Lizzie said about Farnum, and Bruce had to admit that for once she was right.

Now Farnum's great laugh broke out of him. "No, ma'am, they won't clap me into jail. Not with Walt Cronin looking after things."

"Bruce," Susie called. "Come over here and ride with us."

Lizzie started to object, but Jean broke in, "Sure, you go ahead, Bruce," and Lizzie was too worn out to do anything more than grumble.

Dora rode on the seat with her father. There was barely room in the back for Bruce and Susie along with the beef carcass that was covered with a canvas. The Potters had gone on. They'd pick up Frank Evans to ride with Jean. Lizzie had been trying to get them married for a year now, saying they'd all be better off because they could run both places together. That showed how stupid she was, Bruce thought. You didn't make one good farm by putting two poor ones together.

Dusk turned to night before they reached the store.

Bruce and Susie didn't talk. They just sat holding hands, with Dora turning around to see what they were doing every now and then. Bruce didn't like Dora. She was big and coarse, and thought Bruce was a sissy. Maybe he was, the way Dora looked at things, but it wasn't any of her business. Besides, he had his opinion of her. Susie was different. She was small and pretty and sweet, and she didn't have her mind on one thing all the time the way Dora did.

When they went into the store, Lizzie was already at the dry-goods counter. Rose was standing there to wait on her. That always made Lizzie mad. She hated Rose. Besides, she could look without any help from Rose.

Jean and Dora Farnum drifted over to stand beside Lizzie. George Farnum took a look at Walt Cronin's battered face and said, "What happened to you, son?"

"Met up with a bear," Cronin said. "You oughtta see the bear."

"I'll bet," Farnum jeered. "Well, I've got three quarters of a beef in the wagon. Want me to fetch it in?"

"Sure, bring it in."

Lizzie whirled from the counter. "Walt, it's stolen just like all the beef we eat is stolen. There's going to be trouble if we keep this up. Price Regan came to see us today."

"Sure it's stolen," Cronin said, "and we're gonna keep on stealing from these God-damned cowmen until they're busted. This is just a beginning, and don't you worry about Price Regan. He'll be taken care of when the sign's right, and I figure the sign's about right."

Susie kept nudging Bruce with her elbow. He glanced at the jars of candy on the candy counter and wished he had even one nickel to buy some for Susie. She'd never had enough gumdrops in her whole life, but there wasn't any use to ask Sam for money. Lizzie carried the little money the Potters had, and if Bruce asked her for a penny, she'd take his hide off.

Bruce edged toward the door, Susie following, and the

minute they were outside she took his hand and they ran around the store toward the river. They lay down in the grass, and Susie rolled toward him, one leg over his, her mouth coming down for his kiss. Sometimes when she was this way, he thought he'd go crazy, hot and cold at the same time and filled with hungers that confused and frightened him. He sensed that she was tantalizing him, egging him on when she really didn't want him to do anything more than kiss her.

Presently she drew away, whispering, "Bruce, I haven't seen you since Sunday."

"You know the reason," he said. "When I ain't sleeping or eating, I'm working, or Lizzie's gonna know why."

She sighed. "What are we going to do?"

"I know what I'm going to do," he said. "I'm going to run away. I'm done working my tail off for 'em. If I'm going to work as hard as I'm working all the time, I'm going to get paid for it."

"You can't just run off and leave me, Bruce," she said. "You like me, don't you? You like me a little bit?"

"I like you a terrible lot," he said.

"Love" was a word he could never get around to saying. He knew she wanted to hear it, but he couldn't get it out. Now she wiggled against him, whispering, "Bruce, you can come and live with us. Pa wouldn't care. We could make out all right. We always have enough to eat."

"I couldn't do that," he said.

"Why not?"

He hesitated. He didn't want to tell her that he couldn't stand Dora, who'd be watching everything they did and laughing at him. He couldn't tell her, either, that her father was just as shiftless as Lizzie said, and if he didn't steal from Broken Ring or Bridlebit his family wouldn't have enough to eat.

"I just can't," he said. "I'm going away, maybe tomorrow night, but I'll see you before I go."

She kissed him again, believing him. Then they were

silent, both knowing this would be their last evening together. There would be tomorrow afternoon, then he'd be gone and maybe he'd never come back. They both felt like crying, but neither did.

Sixteen was a hell of an age, he thought. You wanted to be a man, but you weren't, and there wasn't any use trying to prove to anybody that you were. It wouldn't be easy getting a job. If he did, he couldn't make enough to support Susie. He didn't know how he'd live. He didn't have a gun. He couldn't bring himself to steal Sam Potter's shotgun. He couldn't even shoot a rabbit to eat.

Time dragged along, Bruce holding her tight in his arms and afraid that each minute would be the last, that Lizzie would come yelling for him that it was time to go. Others from up the Yellow Cat had come, the Wagners and Baileys and Ripleys and the rest.

There was a deal of talking and laughing from the store. The river made a steady roar. A frog croaked from the edge of the stream, and overhead a night bird wheeled against the dark sky and was gone. Then Bruce heard a horse coming along the road. He sat up, pushing the girl away from him.

She whispered, "What is it, Bruce?"

"Somebody's coming," he said. "I'd better tell Cronin."

"Don't go," she begged. "Cronin will find out."

"No, I've got to tell him," he said, and jumped up and ran toward the front of the store, Susie reluctantly following.

When Bruce reached the lighted area in front of the store windows, the rider had pulled up. He saw Bruce and called, "Kid, tell Cronin I've got a calf for him."

Bruce recognized Curly Blue's voice. Blue had been here often, just as a number of cowboys had. Bruce couldn't understand this business, stealing from their own outfits, and he had a hunch that Cole Weston and the rest of the ranchers wouldn't believe it if they were told.

"Get a move on, kid," Blue said.

Bruce went inside and pushed through the crowd until he reached Cronin. He said, "Walt, Blue's outside with a calf. He wants you."

Cronin slapped him on the back. "Thanks, son." He winked at George Farnum. "Business is still good." He called, "Rose," and motioned toward the door. "Curly's outside. Tell him to put the calf in the barn."

Rose nodded and went out. There was a moment of uneasy silence, Bruce backing toward the door. Then Lizzie said, "Walt, you're a fool. I told you Price Regan was out here today. All he needs is for somebody like Curly Blue to swear what's going on."

No one but Lizzie would have had the temerity to talk to Cronin that way. He glared at her, making it plain he didn't like it, then he said, "Miz Potter, you pay attention to your knitting and I'll pay attention to mine. It's boys like Curly Blue who make our business safe. We're all in the same boat. That's why nobody's gonna tell nothing on nobody else."

But that kind of logic didn't appeal to Lizzie. "It'll get us all killed, you mean." She pointed an accusing finger at Cronin, her thin face red with fury. "You've been flaunting the law of God and man, and now it's going to catch up with you. Don't forget I told you, neither." She took Jean by the arm and nodded at her husband. "We're going home. Get into the wagon, Bruce."

She sailed out, leaving an uneasy silence behind her. Bruce saw Susie standing at the corner of the building, but he didn't go to her.

Chapter 8

PRECISELY AT EIGHT O'CLOCK PRICE REGAN, SHAVED, bathed, and then smelling of Cologne water, rang the bell of the Madden house. He had not seen Laura or her father since morning, and it would not have surprised him if Barry Madden had met him at the door and said he wasn't welcome.

He was surprised when Madden opened the door and said genially, "Good evening, Price. Laura will be ready in a few minutes." For a moment Price studied the man, taken aback by this greeting, but he found no hint of anger or resentment in either Madden's face or voice. He stepped into the hall, thinking that Laura always had a way of getting around her father and that she must have done it again.

Madden shut the door and led the way along the hall, saying, "Come on back to the study. We'll have a drink while we're waiting for Laura."

The parlor in the front of the house had been expensively furnished for Laura's mother. Here she had entertained the elite of Elk River Valley. After she had died,

Laura had taken over the parlor for her parties.

Barry Madden hated these social occasions, and he put in only as much of an appearance as propriety required. The study in the back was his room with its great fireplace and oak paneling and the dark, somber furniture. He always kidnapped as many men as he could from Laura's parties and took them to his study for a drink, a few off-color stories, and some sober talk about the future of the west end of Tremaine County, if Laura permitted him to keep them there that long.

Now, when Madden threw the door of the study open and motioned for Price to step past him, Price stood absolutely still, shocked into immobility, and yet he knew at once he shouldn't have been. This was typical of Barry Madden. Here were Cole Weston, the Mohawk brothers, and Red Sanders.

In a corner behind Weston stood Max Harker, the usual cynical grin on his thin face. He wanted to give the impression he was a spectator, not a participant, but Price knew that if he actually thought that, he was fooling no one but himself. He was a part of Madden's scheming or he wouldn't be here.

Price stepped inside, nodding a greeting. The cowmen nodded back, making no effort to hide their hostility. Harker said, "Good evening, Deputy," the grin still on his lips as if he were enjoying in anticipation the scene that was certain to come.

Madden moved to the table, motioning to the decanter that was there. He asked, "You'll have a drink, won't you, Price?"

"Not tonight," Price said, and added by way of explanation, "I'll be with Laura in a few minutes."

Madden paused, uncertain as to the next move. Price stood stiffly by the door, gaze touching Cole Weston, then moving to the others.

The Mohawk brothers were identical twins with coarse dark hair and hawk noses and sailboat ears, their skin so swarthy that Price suspected they were half Mexican.

The only way Price could tell them apart was by the scar Joe had high on his right cheek. If there was talking to be done, Joe did it. Price couldn't remember hearing Tom say ten words since he'd been in Saddle Rock. Both were bachelors, probably in their late thirties, and from what Price had seen and heard, they were as tough and brutal a pair of men as he'd ever run into, with no room in them for gentleness.

The weakest of the four was Red Sanders, but the weakness was not a lack of physical courage. Rather, the way Price judged him, it was a willingness to live and let live, a reluctance to take the kind of direct action that Cole Weston advocated. Sanders had a wife and two children in whom he took great pride, and he was different from the other three, too, in that he liked to laugh, his broad horse teeth much in evidence.

These four made up what Cole Weston called the Cowmen's Council. In the past they had been able, with Madden's help, to make their collective will the law on Elk River regardless of what the former deputies in Saddle Rock thought or did. But Price Regan was not like the deputies who had preceded him, and he wondered how much his presence in Saddle Rock had held Weston and the others back these last months. Now, as his gaze returned to Weston, he had a feeling that the time of holding back was gone. What had happened this morning seemed ample proof of that.

The seconds ribboned out until Madden showed his embarrassment. It was evident he didn't know quite how to approach this, but finally he cleared his throat.

"Price, we wanted to have a little talk with you before you left this evening with Laura. About the problem we briefly discussed this morning."

Madden cleared his throat again, and added hastily, "We carry a good deal of influence with the legislature, Cole especially. We're sure that the next session will cut Elk River Valley off from Tremaine County and organize it as a separate county. Like I told you this morning, you'd be our first sheriff. We were just discussing it. We agreed you'd make a damned good one."

Price grinned. This wasn't what they'd been discussing at all. He said, "That's right kind of you."

"Tell him, Barry," Weston snapped. "God damn it, tell him, or I will."

Madden took a step back from the table, his hands shoved into his pants' pockets. "There's this other thing we talked about this morning. You know, Cronin and that woman of his. You've got to get rid of them."

Price pinned his gaze on Weston's bearded face. He said, "Cole, you ought to know by now that as long as I'm deputy, you'll answer to something higher than your law."

Weston gave Madden a bare half-inch nod. "I told you that you'd waste our time, Barry."

"Now let's not jump the gun . . ." Madden began.

"I'll make myself clear to all of you," Price broke in. "I think you're right about Cronin. He refuses to explain where he got his calves and he's proddy as hell. Acts like he wants a fight, but that's not the point. My job is to find sound evidence that he's either been stealing or receiving stolen property. If he's been receiving it, who's doing the stealing?"

"Well, by God, Regan, you must have more sense than you act like you've got," Weston said. "There's a dozen thieving nester families on the Yellow Cat. You don't need to look no farther."

"I may be a little short of brains," Price said, "but maybe you are, too. If you're losing calves like you claim, you ought to know that the settlers on the Yellow Cat don't have the guts or the savvy to cross the river to Rocking C range and steal anything of yours. Bridlebit and Broken Ring, yes. Rocking C, no."

"Makes sense," Red Sanders agreed. "They're a yellow, no-good bunch."

"I'm losing calves, all right," Weston said. "Cronin must be doing it himself."

Price shook his head. "No. Rose is quite an attraction. Some of your cowboys could be swapping a calf for services rendered."

Weston threw out a big hand in a violent gesture. "Not any of my boys. Get this straight, Regan. You've been crawfishing too long. We've waited as long as we're going to. Move Cronin and that woman tonight."

"I'll move them when I get the evidence I need," Price said. "No sooner."

"To hell with the evidence!" Weston said angrily. "Tonight. You understand?"

"No, I don't," Price said, "and you don't, either. Now there's something else we'd better talk about. I've heard how you four have handled settlers who tried to locate on Elk River. It happened before my time, but I've heard it so often it must be true. Men were shot. Two were lynched. Cabins burned. That's against the law, too. If you hadn't done it, the nesters wouldn't be on the Yellow Cat now. They'd be on Elk River where they could make a living farming and wouldn't have to steal."

Weston's temper was close to the boiling point. "Regan, are you accusing me . . ."

"Of course I'm accusing you. Who else would do it? I'll arrest you as quick as I would Walt Cronin if I find out that you've broken the law."

"Maybe you've never heard my side of it," Weston said. "I'll explain it once and only once. I'm the man who opened up this country. I came here not long after the Union Pacific was built across southern Wyoming. I drove in a herd of cattle with a handful of men, and me and my wife started keeping house in a cabin made of cottonwood logs. We ran the risk of being massacred just like Meeker was. We fought rustlers and we hung some of 'em. We depended on ourselves because we had to. Everything we couldn't make we hauled in from Rawlins. Have you got enough sense to understand what I'm telling you?"

"Is that all?" Price asked.

"No, by God, it ain't!" Weston shouted. "Can you get it through your thick head that I'm not asking for anything I don't deserve? You call it justice for men like Cronin and them settlers on the Yellow Cat to come in now when it's safe because I made it safe and steal our stock? You call it justice to let 'em stay when you know that their staying is an invitation for every other lazy bastard in the country to move in here and settle?"

"Sometimes it's a little hard to know what justice is," Price conceded, "but you're wrong on one point. You are asking for more than you deserve. The land up the Yellow Cat and down Elk River is public domain, and people have a right to claim it and farm it. But if you drive them off that land, then you're outside the law and I'll arrest you. As far as Cronin and the settlers are concerned, I've told you and I'll keep on telling you that I'll arrest any or all of them the minute I get the deadwood on them."

Price turned toward the door and was reaching for the knob when Max Harker called, "Price." As he turned, Harker said, "Looks to me like you just lost your marshal's star. I told you that you'd better crawl."

"I'm not one to crawl for a marshal's star or anything else," Price said.

Weston's restraint was lost now. He raised a fist and shook it at Price. "I've wanted to get rid of you before now, Regan. The only reason I didn't was on account of Barry, who kept asking for more time so you could get some sense in your head, but you've used up your time. You've refused to do your duty, so we'll do it for you."

"You?" Price said. "Or some plug ugly like Curly Blue and gunslingers like Pete Nance?"

"Us," Weston snapped. "Me and Red and Tom and Joe. If you interfere, you're a dead man. You haven't got a friend left. Not even Barry."

Price glanced at Madden and saw that Weston was right. He said, "I've never refused to do my duty. Fact is, I've been telling you I will. Just be sure it's not you, Cole, who goes to the county seat for trial instead of Walt Cronin."

He went out, Weston blasting him with a volley of oaths. He smiled grimly as he went along the hall. It was in the open at last. What had been said with Barry Madden in the bank this morning was only a warning to what had been said just now. Weston would not retreat. He was incapable of it.

Laura was waiting for him in the parlor. The instant she saw him, she cried, "We had a date for eight o'clock, but is it me you want to see? It doesn't look like it, going back there with Daddy while I cool my heels waiting on you. If I'm going to be your wife, it seems to me I ought to come first once in a while."

He looked down at her flushed and angry face, realizing more than ever how much he loved her. Suddenly he was sick with a sense of frustration, sick with the burden that all lawmen must face if they keep their jobs, sick with the choice he must make.

"I'm sorry, Laura," he said. "Sorrier than I can tell you. Right now it looks like you won't be my wife."

The anger died in her at once. She gripped his arms, asking, "What happened, Price? Tell me."

He hesitated, glancing back along the hall, then he stepped into the parlor and, taking her hands, pulled her to him. "I should have told you a long time ago. I would have, I guess, if I hadn't been so afraid I'd lose you."

She shut the door and led him to the orange love seat on the other side of the room. She sat down and pulled him to the seat beside her. "Maybe I can understand. I'll try, Price. It's part of a wife's job to understand, and all I really want to do is to be a good wife."

He sensed that at this moment she was a woman, serious and competent, and not the willful and prankish girl who had got him out of bed that morning to go to the bank and see her father. He said, "You've been wanting to get married for a month, but I've been putting you off. It wasn't just that we didn't have a house to live in. It was more than that. You see, Ralph Carew knew that trouble was shaping up over here. That's why he sent me to Saddle Rock. I shouldn't have asked you to marry me until it was settled."

"And now you're trying to say we can't get married until it's settled?"

"That's it," he said. "I'm in a pinch because I'm alone. Both sides hate me. If I could shut my eyes, or run, I'd be all right, but I can't do either. So it looks like my plow's going to get cleaned. If we got married tomorrow, you might be a widow on Monday."

"Price, you fool," she whispered. "I knew that all the time. If we waited until this trouble was over, there'd just be more. Why, we'd never get married if that was our reason for waiting."

He had been a fool, he thought. She understood far more than he had guessed, and he should have talked to her about it. Still, there was this gap between him and Barry Madden, a gap that had widened until now he saw no way to bridge it.

"But your dad . . ." he began.

"Price, it's me you're marrying, not Daddy. This morning when I went into the bank, he was so mad at you he wouldn't even talk about it, but if it has to be a choice between you, then it's you. He knows that." She chewed on her lower lip a moment, her eyes searching his face, then she added: "About your running away or closing your eyes. If you could do either one, I wouldn't love you. Maybe I will be a widow on Monday, but I'd rather have one day as your wife than never be your wife at all."

He got up and drew her to her feet. He saw that her lips were trembling, that her eyes were shining in a way he had never seen them shine before. A girl-wife at times, perhaps, but a woman-wife when it counted.

"I love you, Laura," he said. "You set the wedding day. Maybe it'll have to be a hotel room for a few days, but we'll make out." He kissed her, her arms clutching him with fierce, unyielding strength. When he let her go, he said, "I'm sorry I kept you waiting, but there are times when a man's job comes ahead of the wife he loves."

"I know, Price. I shouldn't have said what I did."

He grinned at her. "Well, we're all dressed up. Why don't we go to that dance?"

Chapter 9

USUALLY BRUCE JARVIS WAS PERMITTED TO SLEEP A LITTLE later on Sundays than on weekdays, but not this Sunday morning. Lizzie Potter shook him awake with the sun barely up. "Get dressed. I've got a chore for you to do."

Bruce burrowed deeper into the covers, his first thought one of dismal regret that he hadn't run away last night. Lizzie yanked the blankets off him and gave him a slap on the rump. "Get up or I'll whop you good."

He sat up, rubbing his eyes and yawning, and looked at Lizzie, who was still wearing her nightgown, her hair down her back in long braids. God, how he hated her! Six years of being a slave, and he'd never had as much as a kind word. He wished he'd run away the first night the Potters had taken him. And he'd thought he was getting a home!

"Hitch up the wagon and go to the store," Lizzie said. "I need a sack of sugar. I aimed to get it last night, but I was so mad at Walt Cronin when I left the store that I clean forgot it."

Bruce pulled on his pants. "Walt ain't gonna like it, me getting him up this early."

"Get him up anyhow," Lizzie snapped. "Have him put it on tick."

Cronin wouldn't like that, either, but there wasn't any sense in telling Lizzie. She'd cuss Cronin and maybe slap Bruce, and he could be sure of only one thing. He wouldn't get any money.

He pulled on his socks and shoes, and picked up his battered hat from the corner of the room where he'd thrown it last night. He went out into the sharp morning air and harnessed up the team. In an hour or so it would be warm and in another hour so downright hot he couldn't stand it, but now it was just plain cold. He wished he'd brought his coat. Well, it wasn't worth going back for. He'd just get a tongue lashing from Lizzie.

He stepped into the seat, glancing at the saddle horse that was in the corral back of the barn. For a moment he was tempted to take the horse and start out now. He shook his head. Lizzie would probably see him. Besides, he wanted to talk to Susie again before he left. Anyhow, it was just common sense to put as many miles between him and the Yellow Cat as fast as he could before the Potters discovered he'd taken the horse.

He drove out of the yard, Lizzie coming to the door to see why he hadn't started sooner. She sure was a driving woman, he thought. He admired Jean for having enough courage to silence her mother, and although he despised Sam for letting his wife run over him he did wish he had been able to work up the immunity to Lizzie's tirades that Sam had. He just went about his business and let her run off at the mouth, acting as if he actually didn't hear.

But Bruce had not been able either to silence Lizzie or to develop an immunity, so for him escape was the only solution. He looked forward to it with relief, but the pleasure of anticipation was balanced by the knowledge he would never see Susie again.

So he drove along, daydreaming about her kisses and how it had been last night, lying in the grass with her, wanting her and afraid to do anything. There was still this afternoon. He'd tell her he loved her. He'd promise to send for her. Or come back as soon as he had a little money. He'd make all the promises she wanted. And then . . . After that he drove along, lost in the boldness of his dreams.

When Bruce reached the store, he drove around to the back because Cronin slept in a small leanto room and he'd still be in bed. Bruce wondered if he'd branded the calf Curly Blue had brought. Probably he'd done it before he'd gone to bed. He wouldn't take any chances of some outsider finding an unbranded calf in his barn, especially since that deputy Regan had been nosing around again.

Bruce tied the lines around the brake handle and got down. The air had warmed up in just the time it had taken him to drive to the store. He glanced at the sky. Blue, without the slightest stain of a cloud except the ones that lay in the pockets high among the peaks of the Singing Wind Range.

He pounded on Cronin's door, hoping he'd be asked to stay for breakfast and knowing he wouldn't. By the time he got back, the Potters would have had their breakfast and he wouldn't get anything until dinner when the neighbors got there. He'd have to listen to Sam mumble through the scripture and a sermon, and then it would be another hour before they had the food spread out. By the time he got a chance to eat, he'd be so hungry he couldn't get enough inside him to satisfy him.

He rapped on the door again, and he heard Cronin's sleepy, "What do you want?"

"It's Bruce Jarvis. Lizzie sent me to get a sack of sugar." Silence. Maybe Cronin had gone back to sleep. Bruce hammered on the door again. "I'm sorry, Walt, but you know how Lizzie is. I can't go back till I get that sugar."

Cronin opened the door. He yawned and stretched, and knuckled his eyes, and then sat down on the side of the bed and yawned again.

"Yeah, sonny, I know how Lizzie is. I sure feel sorry for you. I can't think of nothing worse than living with that old bitch."

He pulled on his pants and boots. "Come on, boy. I'll get your sugar and you can get to hell out of here and I'll go back to bed."

He led the way through a door into the storeroom. Several sacks of sugar were piled against the wall. Cronin looked at them and then at Bruce. "I suppose she wants a whole sack. Did you fetch any money?"

"No."

Bruce hesitated, thinking that Sam was the one settler on the Yellow Cat who had been reasonably successful at staying clear of the stealing that gave the rest a living. If it had been Frank Evans or George Farnum or any of the others, he could have said there'd be a calf along in a few days, but he couldn't say that about Sam, so he said, "Lizzie told me to have you put it on tick."

"Put it on tick," Cronin mimicked. "Well, by God, I suppose she thinks I'm in the charity business. You tell her I won't get to the county seat for supplies for a month. I can't spare a full sack." He went into the store, nodding for Bruce to follow. "I've got part of a sack that'll have to do her."

Bruce followed as far as the gun rack and stood there admiring the rifle and shotguns and six-shooters. Cronin found a sack of sugar that was less than half full, and carried it to where Bruce stood.

"How do you like that .32–.40?" Cronin asked. "It ain't a real big gun, but it shoots mighty good."

Bruce picked it up and ran a hand lovingly down the barrel.

"It's a beauty, Walt. It sure is."

"How'd you like to have it?"

"Aw, you're joshing, Walt. I don't have no money."

"I know you don't," Cronin said. "Getting money out of Lizzie Potter is like trying to get some fun out of an old maid, but I wasn't joshing. How old are you?"

"Going on seventeen."

"You tied down to the Potters in any way? Kinfolks or anything?"

"No," Bruce answered bitterly. "I just work my butt off for 'em."

"That's the way I figured it. I'll tell you what, Bruce. I need help now and then. I've got to get Rose out of the store. She won't like it, but I've got to do it." He grinned. "I'm gonna be in the cattle business in a big way before long, and I'll need help with it. If you want to work for me, I'll give you room 'n board and ten dollars a month." He nodded at the Winchester. "I'll throw that in just to make you feel good."

For a moment Bruce was too choked up to say anything. He had trouble breathing. This was too good to be true. He'd be down here at the store where things happened and not working himself to death on the Potters' farm. He'd be a cowboy, helping Cronin handle his cattle. Then he thought, *I'll be able to see Susie when I want to. Every Saturday night and maybe during the week.*

"Gosh, Walt, I . . ."

"Don't promise me nothing till you think it over," Cronin said. "There's gonna be trouble. I've been getting under some hides or that stinking deputy wouldn't have been here yesterday. That's all right. It's what I want. I hate every God-damned cattleman there is. I came here to fight 'em, and if you work for me, you'll be in the same boat I'm in."

"I ain't afraid of the cattlemen." Bruce swallowed, thinking of Lizzie Potter and what she'd say. He blurted, "I ain't afraid of anybody but Lizzie."

"She can't hurt you except with her tongue." Cronin slapped him on the back. "Then it's a deal, boy. You take the sugar and go tell Lizzie. Leave the wagon with 'em. You can walk back to the store. No, I'll let you take that little sorrel mare. Tie her on behind the wagon—"

He stopped, head cocked. Then Bruce heard the horses

coming on the road from down the river. Cronin ran to a window and looked out. Wheeling, he ran back, grabbed the rifle out of Bruce's hands and began shoving shells into the magazine.

"Get into the back room," he said. "Take the sugar with you. Hide in a corner and stay there no matter what happens. I'm gonna get me some big game in about two minutes."

Cronin was breathing hard, excitement showing in his face. When Bruce didn't move, he shouted, "Jump, damn it!"

Bruce picked up the sugar and ran into the back room. He set the sack down and slipped into a corner and ducked down behind a barrel. He ought to be out there fighting with Cronin, but he had his orders, and when you got orders like that from Walt Cronin you obeyed. Anybody would, he reckoned.

Outside a man yelled, "Open up, Cronin."

"Go to hell," Cronin yelled back. "You poke your head through a window or a door and I'll blow it off."

There was more talk, obscene and threatening, and Bruce was listening so hard he didn't realize anyone had come in through the back until the man was opposite him and he had no time to warn Cronin. Bruce didn't know him, but he didn't know any of the cattlemen except a few of the cowboys like Curly Blue who came to see Rose. This fellow was tall and slender with red hair. Even in the gloom of the back room, Bruce got a good look at him and knew he'd recognize him if he ever saw him again.

The rancher moved past Bruce and went on into the store. He said, "Put the Winchester down, Cronin. Make a fast move and you're a dead man."

Bruce couldn't see what was happening, but from the racket he had a good idea what was going on. Cronin apparently was being forced to open the front door. There was a struggle, some banging around and cursing, then a man said in a voice of authority, "Tie his hands behind him, Red. Tom, got that rope ready?"

"You bet," another man said. "It'll fit his neck, all right."

"Then fetch him along," the man with the authoritative voice said. "What's the matter with you, Red? You're looking kind of puny?"

"I feel puny," the redhead said. "I don't like this, Cole. We didn't give him a trial or nothing. Let's warn him and turn him loose."

"Trial?" The other man laughed. "You figure a cow thief deserves a trial? Fetch him along, Tom. He's going to be a warning, all right. Every settler on the Yellow Cat will get the idea, and be out of the country in twenty-four hours."

Cronin might have been knocked out, but he had his voice now, and he cursed them and called them yellow. "Every stinking damned bastard that raises cows is the same bitching breed of dogs. They murdered my parents in Wyoming and now you're fixing to murder me. You don't have the guts to give me a gun and—"

"He's right," the man with the red hair said. "This is murder."

That was all the talk Bruce could hear. They must have dragged Cronin out through the front door. Bruce told himself he could save Cronin. All he had to do was to get a gun off the rack in the store and load it and start shooting. They weren't fooling. They aimed to hang him, all right.

Bruce got up and grabbed the top of the barrel to keep from falling. Then his knees gave way and he did fall. A voice seemed to be telling him he hadn't shot a gun half a dozen times in his life. He couldn't hit any of the lynchers if he tried. They'd kill him. He wouldn't do any good. But he had to try. He got up again and held to the top of the barrel, the room whirling in front of him.

He had never known fear before, nothing worse than the fear of Lizzie Potter's flaying tongue, not this kind of fear that turned his insides to jelly and sent these terrible chills up and down his spine.

Presently the room stopped whirling. Still he stood

there, sweat dripping down from his face. He lost all track of time. It might have been seconds or minutes before he could make his legs carry him into the store where he picked up a rifle.

He fumbled among the boxes of shells until he found the right ones and filled the magazine. He stuck the box into his pocket and went out through the back room, still sweating, still trembling, but able now to make his body answer the orders his brain gave.

Cronin's leanto room was built against one half of the main building. Bruce had pulled his team and wagon into this corner, and it wasn't until later that he realized that the position of the team and wagon had saved his life.

When he peeked around the end of the leanto, he saw he was too late. The cowmen were riding off, downriver, and Walt Cronin's body swung from a cottonwood limb, his head cocked at a horrible grotesque angle. From where the cowmen had been they could not have seen the team and wagon. But the redhead had come in through the back and must have seen them.

Terror was in Bruce again. He stared at the body, swinging a little in the hot wind that blew up the valley, and thought that if he'd been discovered he'd be hanging beside Cronin. But they might come back. The redhead might remember about the team and wagon.

Suddenly he was sick. He bent over and retched, but there was nothing in his stomach to come up. For a time his whole body quivered with this agony, and when it passed he could do nothing except lean against the wall.

He heard a woman scream from in front of the store building. Rose! There was nothing he could do now. He had waited too long, giving way to fear. His first real test of manhood, and he had failed.

He threw the rifle into the bed of the wagon and climbed into the seat. He whirled the horses away from the building, slashing them with the end of the lines, and went rocketing into the road and on up the Yellow Cat.

As he went past Rose's cabin, he saw her in front, wearing nothing but her nightgown, her hair down her back, one scream after another coming from her open mouth.

Bruce had never driven horses crazy hard as he did this morning. Frank Evans heard him as he flashed past and ran out of his barn and yelled. Bruce didn't stop. When he reached the Potter place and pulled the lathered, heaving horses to a stop in the yard, they were waiting for him, Lizzie screaming what was the matter with him, Jean pale-faced, and Sam running to the horses and putting his hands on their sweat-gummed bodies.

"Cronin," Bruce said hoarsely. "They hanged him."

The Potters stood motionless, staring at him. It was natural that Lizzie would be the first to speak, and what she said was natural, too. "He's been flaunting the laws of God and man, and now he's harvested the crop he sowed."

Sam and Jean condemned her with their eyes. Sam asked, "How did it happen?"

Bruce told them as well as he could, as if it had been a terrible nightmare that had wakened him in the middle of a black, lonely night.

When he finished, Jean asked, "You didn't know them?"

"No. I never seen them before."

"But you'd know them if you saw them again?" Jean pressed.

"I'd sure know the redhead."

"That was Sanders," Sam said. "Owns Bridlebit."

"You didn't get a look at the others?" Jean asked.

"No, but one of 'em was called Cole. Another one Tom."

"Cole Weston," Sam said bitterly. "Tom would be Tom Mohawk. I reckon the fourth one would be his brother Joe. They wouldn't leave a job like this to their hands. They was gonna see it was done right."

Silence a moment, then Lizzie asked, "Where's the sugar?"

Nobody paid any attention to her. Sam said, "We've got to get word to Price Regan. Bruce's testimony will hang all four of 'em."

"Pa." Jean shook his arm. "Bruce says Sanders came in through the back. He must have seen the team and wagon, and after awhile he'll think of it. Would he recognize the horses?"

"Reckon he would," Sam answered. "He seen me in town with 'em, and once he ran onto me when I was on top cutting cedar posts and he gave me a cussing for it."

"Then they'll come here," Jean said. "When they find Bruce, they'll kill him."

"If they don't find him, they'll kill us for hiding him," Lizzie cried. "Get him out of here! I don't aim to get shot on his account."

Again Jean and Sam ignored her. Of the four, only Jean was thinking straight. She said, "Pa, saddle Nip for Bruce. I'll fix him a sack of grub. He's got to hide out for a while."

Jean raced into the house while Sam ran toward the corral, calling, "Come on, Bruce! You've got to stay hid out for a spell, then you ride in at night, careful like, and I'll tell you what's happened."

Lizzie remained where she was, pale and trembling, and confused by the fact that no one was paying the least attention to her. By the time the horse was saddled, Jean had returned with a flour sack of food. Sam tied it behind the saddle. Jean said, "I'll take the wagon and go to town and tell Regan."

Bruce put a foot into a stirrup and pulled himself into the saddle. He said, "Even if Sanders did recognize the team, I don't know why he'd think it was me in the store. Chances are they'll figure it was Sam . . ."

"I'll tell them!" Lizzie screamed. "If they come nosing around here, I'll tell them. I'm not going to lose my husband on account of something you done." As Jean started to drive away, Lizzie called, "Jean, don't you fetch that deputy out here."

"Get moving, Bruce," Sam said. "Remember now. Stay hid out."

Bruce rode off, following the wagon that soon disappeared through the narrows between the Potter and Evans farms. Lizzie yelled, "Don't you come back here with your tail between your legs looking for help, Bruce Jarvis. You just keep on going."

He was still too dazed to think straight, but he knew he'd better do what she said and keep going. Maybe Sam could keep Lizzie from telling Sanders and the rest of them that he was the one who had been in the store, but he doubted it. There wasn't much that Sam ever kept Lizzie from doing, once she made up her mind.

When Bruce reached the narrows, he remembered that the rifle he had taken from the store was still in the wagon. He wished he had it. He kept seeing Cronin hanging from that limb, Cronin who had wanted to be his friend and who had offered him a job. Bruce kept telling himself he could have saved Cronin. He hadn't tried in time.

Without conscious thought, he crossed the creek and left the horse behind an upthrust of rock. He couldn't ride. He couldn't do anything. He slid out of the saddle, leaving the reins dangling, and lay down on the ground and cried as he had not cried since his parents had died.

Chapter 10

WHEN PRICE WAS IN TOWN SUNDAY MORNING, HE MADE IT A practice to call at the Madden house at 10:45 to take Laura to church. Usually her father went with them. As Price rang the bell this morning, he fervently hoped Barry Madden was going anywhere but to church. His hopes were immediately dashed, for Madden, dressed in his Sunday best, opened the door.

"Come in, Price," Madden said. "I think Laura is almost ready."

They waited in the hall, silence a barrier between them, Madden's face very grave. Price glanced at him and turned his gaze away, wondering, as he had a good many times, how far the banker would go in backing Cole Weston. Apparently they had gone down the line together so far, but last night Weston had made his intentions clear. The ruthless brutality which characterized the rancher did not seem to be in Madden. If they could be separated . . .

His thoughts were broken into by Laura, who came down the stairs, wearing a sailor hat and a prim blue dress which gave her an oddly subdued appearance. It was for Sunday morning only, Price thought, an appearance which she would shed when she returned home as easily as she would take off the dress.

"Good morning, darling," Laura said, and paused halfway down the stairs for him to admire her.

The spot where she stopped was carefully chosen. The morning sunlight, pouring through the stained glass of an east window, touched her with the colors of a rainbow. Price smiled, thinking this bit of vanity was quite apart from the demure Sunday-morning manner she assumed.

"You're beautiful," he said. "As beautiful as an angel with the glory of the Lord upon her."

"A very pretty compliment," she said, and came on down the stairs. "I thank you for it."

Madden snorted. "She sure fooled you. She's no angel. If you'd heard her talk to me at breakfast, you'd know she wasn't."

"You deserved it," she said. "Anyhow, Price wouldn't want to marry an angel."

"I'm surprised she even looks like one," Madden said, "with you keeping her up all night dancing."

Price kissed her, being careful not to disturb her hat that was perfectly placed atop her curls. As she went out with Price, she said, a little spitefully, "It's better to look like an angel on Sunday than act like the devil."

Her father said nothing to that. He closed the door behind her and Price, and they moved slowly toward the church through the hot morning sunlight, Laura walking between Price and her father. Something had happened, Price thought, for he felt the barbed edge of their hostility toward each other. Later he would learn what it was, but he couldn't ask now.

The church service dragged unbearably. Now and then Price glanced at Laura, who sat with her hands folded decorously on her lap, a set smile on her face; then he looked past her at Barry Madden, whose face was more grim than Price had ever seen it. He knew it was wishful thinking, but he couldn't keep from hoping that Laura would prove to be the lever by which Madden could be pried free from Weston and his friends.

Price stood up with relief while the final hymn was sung, then the preacher lifted his hand and gave the benediction. He had barely said, "Amen," when the sound of running horses and the rattle of a wagon came to Price, then a woman's voice, "Regan! Regan!"

Price ran down the aisle and out through the door, forgetting the dignity of the place and time. Jean Potter jumped down from the wagon seat, hurrying past the lathered horses. She cried, "Regan, they hanged Walt Cronin this morning!"

Price stood motionless, shocked by what he had heard, yet at the same time he realized this was exactly what he had expected. He even had warned Cronin that he'd better leave the country, but Cronin had not been capable of taking a warning.

The congregation ran outside behind Price, the preacher with them. All of them were shocked into immobility, just as Price had been. He walked to the girl, asking, "Do you know who did it?"

Before she could answer, Barry Madden rushed up, saying, "You don't know for sure, do you, Miss Potter? You weren't there when it happened, were you?"

Price glanced at Madden, realizing he shouldn't be surprised at this interference, either. It must have been decided last night. Barry Madden looked as guilty as hell. Price thought, *He knew exactly what was going to happen.*

Price shoved him back with a thrusting elbow. "Do you know who did it?"

The girl was almost hysterical. Tears were in her eyes, she was trembling, and her face was so pale she looked as if she were about to faint. Finally she said in a barely audible voice, "No, I wasn't there. I don't know for sure who did it."

Laura tugged at Price's elbow. "I'll take her home. She ought to lie down."

"All right, take care of her. I'll be along in a minute."
Price swung to face Madden. "You let her alone, Barry.
Understand?"

Madden nodded as Laura walked away with Jean.
Madden said, "I've never been sure whether you had a
thimbleful of brains or not, but looks like I'm going to
find out."

Price walked away. He had to or he'd have lost his
temper. The preacher called, "Is there anything I can do?
Or any of us? Cronin didn't have any family, did he?"

"No." You couldn't call Rose his family, Price
thought. The preacher, of course, would ignore her
anyway. "I'll see the body's brought to town. You can
give Cronin a Christian burial."

Price stepped into the wagon and drove away. The
preacher stared after him, confused and speechless. Mrs.
De Long came to him and said. "You can't hold funeral
services for a man like that, can you, Mr. Dolan? Not
here in the church, anyhow."

Price left the team at the livery stable. "Barney, soon
as you get these horses rubbed down, harness up another
team to the wagon. Walt Cronin was lynched this morning. I want you to go help me cut the body down and
fetch it into town."

Barney De Long, the liveryman, backed away. "No,
Mr. Regan, I ain't having no part of that kind of
business. I can't get away today . . ."

"By God, you'll go!" Price grabbed a fistful of De
Long's shirt. "I'll deputize you if it'll make you feel any
better, and I'll twist your skinny neck if I have to. I won't
be gone more'n half an hour. When I get back, you'd
better have that team ready to go."

He wheeled and sprinted down the runway and out
into the street, feeling the urgency of time. It was too late
to save Cronin, but Rose might still be alive. If there was
any evidence left at the scene of the hanging, he'd have to
get there ahead of everyone else or it would be tramped
out. But maybe no one else would be there. The settlers

up the Yellow Cat wouldn't. They'd be milling around like a bunch of sheep. Walt Cronin had been the only leader they had.

Price took a minute in his hotel room to change clothes, then he buckled his gun belt around him and, picking up his Winchester, left the hotel and hurried to the Madden house. He found Jean lying on the couch, still pale but reasonably composed.

"She'll be all right," Laura said. "She was just excited. I guess anybody would be who had to bring news like that."

"It was seeing him," Jean said. "I took just one look, and that was all, but I'll dream about him the rest of my life."

Barry Madden was not in sight. Price asked, "Where's your dad, Laura?"

"I don't know," she said. "He didn't come home after church." She put a hand to her throat, frightened eyes on Price. "What does it mean? What's going to happen?"

"I don't know, except that some people will get hurt, and your dad may be among 'em." He sat down beside the couch. "How did you know about it?"

Jean sat up. She put a hand to her forehead as if hoping it would help her think, then she said, "I'd like to talk to you alone, Mr. Regan."

"I'll fix some coffee," Laura said, and disappeared into the kitchen.

As soon as she was gone, Jean told Price what had happened. Then she added, "It's Bruce I'm worried about, Mr. Regan. He's always had a hard time. Ma never treated him good. It's too bad he was the one who had to be there when it happened. He's afraid of Ma. Maybe he'll never come back, but if he runs away they'll find and kill him." She lowered her head, fighting her tears, then she asked miserably, "Men like that would kill him if they found him, wouldn't they?"

Price thought about Cole Weston, then about the Mohawk brothers. Only Red Sanders would have a weak stomach about things like that, and he'd be overridden by the others. "Yeah, they'd kill him," Price said, "if they knew he was there, but maybe they won't know that."

"They'll hear," Jean said. "Ma gabs all the time. Soon as the neighbors come today, she'll tell them the whole story. Mr. Regan, can you find Bruce?"

"It depends," he said. "I'll try. That's all I can promise. Now there's one thing I want you to go back over. Bruce was hiding in a corner of the storeroom when a man came in through the back. This man had red hair?"

She nodded. "That's right. Bruce don't know any of the cattlemen except a few of the cowboys like Curly Blue who bring calves to trade to Cronin. He—"

"Wait a minute. You say some of the Rocking C cowboys brought calves to trade to Cronin. You're sure of that?"

"Of course. They'd come to drink or play cards." She looked away. "Or to see Rose. I thought you knew."

"How would I know?" he said angrily. "Nobody out there would talk to me. If they had, this wouldn't have happened."

"I'm sorry. I guess we thought you were on the other side."

"I'm not on any side," he said, "but I know what Cronin said about me and I guess your people believed him. Now let's get back to Bruce. He could recognize this redheaded man if he saw him again?"

"Oh, yes. And he heard some of the talk. One man was called Cole. Another one Tom. Pa said it would be Cole Weston and Tom Mohawk, and the other man was probably Joe Mohawk."

Price nodded. "That's likely who it was." He shook his head, realizing that anything Jean or her parents said in court would be hearsay evidence, and that the boy Bruce was the key witness. Weston and the others hadn't known he was there or they wouldn't have ridden off the way they had and left him in the store. They'd kill a boy, all right. Or a woman, either, if it meant saving their hides. He had strong doubts that Rose was alive.

As Price stood up, Jean asked, "You're going to try to do something about this?"

"Of course I'll try, but what I do depends on whether I can find Bruce." He called, "Laura." When she came into the room from the kitchen, he said, "I want Miss Potter to stay with you. I'm going to try to get her folks to come to town. It's too dangerous for them to stay out there. Will you keep them here?"

"Of course, if they'll stay."

"Your dad will raise Cain, but I want to save their lives and I want them where I can put my hands on them." He turned to Jean. "It's important for you to stay here. You'll be safe. Do you understand?"

"Yes." She swallowed with evident effort. "You think my folks are in danger?"

"Yes I do, if Weston and his friends hear about Bruce and that he told you and your folks what he saw."

He left the room, not realizing that Laura had followed him until she called his name. He turned in the doorway as she came to him. He saw the pulse beat in her temples, he felt her hands tremble when she lifted them to his shoulders. She asked, "Price, have you got to go ahead with this? I mean, Cronin being the kind of man he was and all?"

"Yes, I've got to go ahead." He sensed that now, with the showdown at hand, she had little real understanding of the problem he faced, that she was Laura the girl, not Laura the woman. He asked, "Which is the greater crime, stealing calves or taking a human life?"

"Taking a life, of course, but . . ." She was silent a moment, her hands gripping his shoulders, then she said, "It's just that you're alone, Price. You're so terribly alone."

He knew what she meant because he had felt it many times since he'd come to Saddle Rock. Cole Weston controlled the thinking of those who lived on the grass; Barry Madden had almost as complete control over those who lived in town. Again he thought how important it was that Madden and Weston be forced apart, but it was not anything he could say to Laura. She would have to realize it herself.

"I know how much I'm alone," he said, "except for you. I guess it's a good thing this happened before we were married. If you don't want to go ahead with it . . ."

"No, Price, no. I wish we were married now."

He kissed her, letting her feel the desperate need he had of her. Then, their lips parted, he said, "I love you, Laura. I love you very much." He walked away, leaving her standing in the doorway, her eyes following him as long as he was in sight.

De Long had a team hitched to the Potter wagon and Price's roan saddled by the time he reached the stable. Max Harker and Barry Madden were both there, Harker's cynical smile on his thin lips, Madden's face a little red but grimly determined. Embarrassed, Price thought, because he was dead wrong and he knew it.

"I hear Cronin met up with some rope justice," Harker said.

"Rope murder," Price said. "Not justice. No man, even one as big as Cole Weston, has the right to decide justice." Price stepped into the saddle and looked down at Madden.

The banker took a step forward, moistening his lips. He said, "Price, it's like we said in the bank yesterday morning. We don't like each other for exactly the reasons you gave, and I wouldn't be saying this if it wasn't for Laura. I wouldn't have held Weston off this long either. Laura loves you." He spread his hands. "I don't know why, but she does. If you get yourself killed, it's going to be damned hard on her. That's the only reason I'm saying this. Don't pick it up. Let it go. A man like Walt Cronin isn't worth it."

"Barry," Price said, "I'd hate to have on my conscience what you've got on yours." He jerked his head at De Long. "Let's roll."

Price rode through the doorway, the wagon creaking behind him, Madden and Harker standing there staring at him. Harker said, "Funny thing, Barry. I've been dying for ten years and I don't have a damned thing to live for, but I haven't got the guts to do what he's doing. I'd say the odds are about a hundred to one against him."

"Longer'n that," Madden said harshly, "and he doesn't have sense enough to see it."

"Sense?" Harker wasn't smiling now. "No, Barry, you're wrong. He knows. It's not a matter of sense. It's something else, something I wish I had."

Chapter 11

OF THE FOUR MEN WHO TOOK WALT CRONIN OUT OF THE store, only Red Sanders had no part in the hanging. The Mohawk brothers threw the rope over the cottonwood limb, tied Cronin's feet and hands, boosted him into the saddle, then led the horse under the limb and adjusted the noose around Cronin's neck. All the time Cronin was mouthing a volley of oaths and obscenities and threats. He was completely ignored.

When everything was ready, Cole Weston gave the horse a clout with his quirt. The animal plunged out from under Cronin. Sanders watched the man drop, the rope jerking tight under his weight, and heard the limb groan as Cronin's full weight struck it. His neck must have been broken when he fell, for his head twisted at a crazy angle, his mouth fell open, and his eyes bulged from their sockets.

Sanders gigged his horse into motion, turning his head so he wouldn't see the dead man, and rode downstream. The dry wind flowing up the valley touched the cotton-woods and caused their leaves to whisper. Cronin swayed a little in the wind like a ghastly pendulum, the limb making a faint creaking as he swung, but Sanders did not look back.

Over to the west a buzzard was floating with motionless wings above some barren mesa. Before long he'd be here, Sanders thought, stripping meat from the dead man, unless, of course, someone cut him down, but no one would have the nerve to do that, with the possible exception of Price Regan. Sanders wasn't sure about him, but he had a feeling Weston had been underestimating the deputy.

Later, Cole Weston and the Mohawk brothers caught up with Sanders. They rode in silence a long time, traveling downstream to avoid meeting anyone who might be on the road between the store and Saddle Rock.

Presently Weston said with satisfaction, "He'll hang there till he rots. Won't be more'n a few hours till everybody up the Yellow Cat knows what happened. I'm guessing they'll be packing up inside another hour."

"Me'n Tom will take a swing down the creek in a day or so," Joe Mohawk said. "If they ain't moving, we'll bust a few caps. That'll hurry 'em up."

Sanders had always been scared of Weston, partly because he was a young man and a Johnny-come-lately to the Elk River range, whereas Weston had been here for years. It was by his tacit consent that Sanders had started Bridlebit, but more than that was the fact that Weston was a ruthless man who brooked no interference. Sanders had learned long ago that you agreed with him or you had trouble.

This Cronin business had gone against Sanders' grain from the first. He wanted the man moved, all right, and he knew the settlers would follow, but it was Weston's self-centered way of forcing the issue that irritated Sanders. The store and the Yellow Cat were north of the river, and Weston's range lay to the south. It should, then, have been Sanders' and the Mohawks' business, not Weston's, yet Weston had made it his.

Sanders had held his tongue all this time, not agreeing

with Weston, but going along because it was the easiest thing to do. Now, in spite of his resolve not to say or do anything that would anger Weston, he burst out, "We shouldn't have done it, Cole! We should have run him out of the country and let it go at that."

Weston turned his harsh gaze on Sanders. "Well, by God, Red, you're about as stout as a spoonful of whisky in a barrel of rainwater. If it wasn't for me, the clodbusters would have run you clean across the Utah line by now."

Sanders caught the way the Mohawk boys looked at each other. They were just waiting for him to stump his toe. If he was out of the way, they'd move across the Yellow Cat and absorb Bridlebit range, and then they'd be as big as Weston was to the south. Sanders had no illusions about Weston's friendship. He had the big man's support simply because he didn't want the Mohawk brothers to get any bigger than they were. Once Sanders lost that support, he'd be fighting for his life.

"I've got a wife and two kids," Sanders said lamely. "I just don't want them knowing I had any part of this business."

"Didn't notice you taking much part," Weston said.

"Only mistake we made was not stringing that woman up alongside Cronin," Joe Mohawk said. "Chances are she seen us. I say we oughtta go back and do it yet."

"No," Weston snapped. "Nobody would believe her if she did see us. I don't think she did because they sleep late Sundays. I was surprised when we looked in and saw Cronin. I figured we'd catch him in bed. Good thing I thought of sending Red around to the back or we might have had trouble."

"Somebody got him up or he would have been in bed," Sanders said. "There was a team and wagon around at the back."

Weston yanked his horse to a stop. "What'd you say?"

Sanders hadn't intended to mention it, and he mentally cursed himself the instant the words were out of his mouth. He'd been sure someone was hiding in the storeroom, but if he'd rooted the person out and taken him, or her, to Weston, there would have been someone else to hang. One killing was enough, even that of a guilty man. But to have the murder of an innocent person added to Cronin's would have been too much.

Yet, in the back of Sanders' mind the terrifying thought had lingered that he'd been seen, that there had been a witness to the hanging, and that he could be identified. Now, with Weston's condemning stare on him, Sanders realized it was that half-conscious fear which had tripped his tongue.

"There was a team and wagon back of the store," Sanders said finally. "It was pulled in close to the building and we couldn't see it from this side on account of it was hidden by that leanto room of Cronin's."

"Whose was it?" Weston demanded.

"Sam Potter's."

"You see anybody in the back room?"

"No."

"But you didn't look, did you?" Weston said hotly. "By God, Red, we oughtta string you up beside Cronin just for having sawdust in your head instead of brains! You know what you've done?"

"I guess I didn't figure it was important," Sanders said. "You've been telling us all the time not to bother Rose. She sure could have seen the whole business. Besides, I was trying to get in quick so I could get my gun on Cronin."

"You fool!" Weston said bitterly. "You chuckle-headed idiot! It's different with Rose. Hang a woman, even a bitch like that, and you've got folks against you, but going off and leaving a witness who seen the whole thing is . . . is . . ."

He stopped, made incoherent by his anger. Joe Mohawk said, "Looks to me like we've got to go back. Potter might still be there. If he ain't we'll know where to find him."

Weston nodded somber agreement. Sanders said, "Suppose it's Mrs. Potter? Or their girl?"

"We've got to get whoever it was," Weston said. "The whole Potter family if we have to. Wouldn't make much difference if it wasn't for that damned Regan, but if he gets hold of the Potters, he'll raise hell."

They started back, Sanders still arguing, "You just got done saying we can't kill a woman."

"Looks different now," Weston said. "I told you nobody would believe Rose, but they'll believe one of the Potter women, all right."

They rode in silence, the terrifying fear in Sanders that he'd signed his own death warrant the instant he'd mentioned the team and wagon. He glanced at Weston's grim face, then at the Mohawk boys.

He had no chance against the three of them, yet he knew for his own future peace of mind that he couldn't let them kill the Potter women. The Mohawk brothers would do it and not give it a second thought. That was the kind of men they were, but Weston had some principles. Maybe he wouldn't let it happen. A slim hope to cling to, but it was the only hope Sanders had.

When they reached the store, the wagon was gone, as Sanders had known it would be. Joe Mohawk said, "I'm gonna get Rose. I tell you we made a mistake before."

Weston absent-mindedly nodded agreement. After the Mohawk brothers had ridden around the corner of the store, Sanders burst out, "Cole, you can't let the Potter women be killed! Even if it's our necks . . ."

Weston put a hand on his gun and pinned his gaze on Sanders' face. He said ominously, "Red, you haven't had any starch in you from the first and I'm getting mighty damned tired of hearing you talk. If Regan gets his hands on a reliable witness, I tell you, it will be our necks. I don't propose for mine to get stretched. We should have cleaned Regan's plow for him before we called on Cronin."

No use to argue, Sanders thought. Anything he said

would be as useless as waving your bandanna at a runaway horse. Glumly, and with a sense of frustration, he watched Weston get down and kick around in the dirt in back of the store where the team and wagon had been. Then he went inside and came back, shaking his head and cursing Sanders in a bitter monotone.

"You chowder-headed idiot," Weston said. "You sure messed up everything."

"Why didn't you look around yourself?" Sanders demanded.

"I didn't think anyone would be here this time of the morning," Weston said. "Hell, that wasn't the main reason. I trusted you, though why I did I don't know." He swung into the saddle, his fury a devouring flame. "I never will again. You can count on that."

The Mohawk brothers appeared around the corner of the store. Joe said, "She flew the coop. You figure she might be in the store?"

"No, I just looked," Weston said. "She don't worry me. I keep telling you. It's the Potters that'll hang us."

The Mohawks hesitated, the hunger to kill an insatiable appetite in them, but finding Rose would take time, and they knew as well as Weston did that time was what mattered now. Besides, they had not reached the place where they were willing to take a stand against Weston.

Without a word, Weston and the Mohawks started up the road that followed the Yellow Cat, Sanders trailing. He didn't want to go because he knew what would happen. He knew, too, he couldn't stop it if he tried. He wished he'd stayed home; he wished he'd talked to Price Regan before he'd left town last night; he wished . . . But hell, what good were wishes now? He was in just as deep as Weston or the Mohawks. Whatever happened to them would happen to him.

Just below the Evans place Weston reined up and motioned for the others to stop. He got down and studied the road. When he rose, he stared at Sanders with the utmost loathing. "We may be too late," he said.

"If I'm reading the sign right, a wagon's been out and in and out again this morning. It's my guess somebody's gone after Regan."

He mounted and led the way again, turning in at the Evans farm. Joe Mohawk said, "We're wasting time here, Cole."

"No. Whoever went by might have stopped and told him. Better go in and get him."

Tom Mohawk went into the barn, Joe into the house. A moment later Tom's gun roared. He came out of the barn and mounted, saying, "He won't talk."

Joe ran out of the house. "Get him?"

"Got him," Tom said.

"What did he say?" Weston demanded. "Did he know anything?"

Tom seemed surprised. "I didn't ask," he said.

"Don't get into such a hurry when we see the Potters," Weston said. "They've got to talk."

"They'll talk," Joe Mohawk said, and rode on, taking the lead, and to Sanders' surprise, Weston permitted him to do it.

Sanders had trouble thinking coherently. He worked this around in his mind for a time before he thought he understood. For right down sheer cussedness, the Mohawks were far ahead of Weston. Now, with none of his men to back him, Weston lacked the kind of courage it took to hold a tight rein on the Mohawks. Again that terrible feeling of helplessness clawed up through Sanders. Weston, even if he wanted to, could not keep the Mohawks from murdering the Potter family.

Sam Potter was standing in front of his house when the four men turned off the road. As soon as Potter recognized them, he called, "Lizzie, fetch the shotgun."

She ran out of the house and handed her husband the gun just as the four men reined up in front. She said, "Get back on your horse, Mohawk. We don't want nothing to do with you."

"We want to ask some questions, Mrs. Potter," Weston

said smoothly. "Which one of you was at the store this morning?"

"None of us," she cried. "Now get out. Leave us alone."

Both of the Mohawks dismounted and stood on each side of Weston, who remained on his horse. Potter didn't know how to meet this situation, his shotgun swinging from Joe to Tom and back to Joe. They moved slowly and relentlessly toward him, Weston saying, "Better put that scattergun down, Potter."

Lizzie picked up a stick and started after Joe, screaming at him to let them alone. She struck at Joe, but he laughed at her as he caught the descending stick and jerked it out of her hands, then he hit her on the side of the head and knocked her sprawling on the ground in front of the porch.

"I'll kill you for that," Potter said in a hoarse voice.

But Sam Potter was not a man to handle violence, and he hesitated. Weston spurred his horse and drove straight at Potter, who started backtracking as he tried to line the shotgun on Weston. Joe Mohawk, coming on him from the side, grabbed the gun and twisted it out of his hands and threw it halfway to the barn.

Lizzie tried to get up and fell back. Joe Mohawk had his gun in his hand now. He said, "Potter, I'm only going to ask you once. Who was at the store this morning?"

Lizzie screamed, "Don't tell him, Sam! They won't dare kill us."

Potter pressed his lips together and backed up another step. Joe hit him on the side of the head and Potter went down. Joe grabbed him by a shoulder and hauled him to his feet and kicked him in the crotch. Potter screamed in pure agony.

"Answer the question, Potter," Weston said.

"Bruce," Potter whimpered. He was writhing on the grass, out of his head with pain.

"Where's the kid?" Weston demanded.

"He took the saddle horse and ran," Lizzie cried.

"Leave us alone. We don't know nothing about Cronin or who killed him or nothing. Leave us alone."

"Where's the girl?" Weston asked.

"She took the wagon and went to town. Can't you let us alone? Can't you see we ain't hurting nobody and we ain't going to?"

Tom glanced at Weston, who nodded. Tom nodded back and, turning, drew his gun and shot Lizzie in the chest. She fell against the porch, and lay still, her head resting on the lower step. Sam cried out incoherently, the sound like that of a frightened animal, and got to his knees. Tom shot him, first in the shoulder, and when he saw he hadn't hit dead center, he fired again, this bullet slicing through Potter's heart.

Hanging Walt Cronin had been a nightmare to Red Sanders, but this was worse, far worse, something that reached up out of hell. It was time suspended; it was a tiny splinter of eternity that ran on and on without end; it was happening and yet it couldn't be happening.

He saw Lizzie Potter lying with her head cocked on the porch step, blood making a dark streak down the front of her dress. He saw Sam Potter lying motionless on the hard packed dirt of the yard, his blood pumping out of him and spreading on the ground.

A sound came out of Sanders' throat, a sound he never knew he made. He yanked his gun from leather, aiming to kill Tom Mohawk, but he never fired the gun. Weston shot him in the stomach, and Sanders spilled out of his saddle, his horse starting to pitch. Weston shot him again, and all feeling and all knowledge were gone from Red Sanders.

Tom Mohawk stared in surprise at Weston. "The bastard was gonna shoot me."

Weston nodded. "I saw it coming, so I was ready." Then he added briskly, "Tom, get his horse and load him on it. We'll dump him at Evans' place and folks'll think the nesters done it. I'll take a look in the house. Joe, you see about the barn. I reckon the kid and the girl are gone, but we'd better make sure. If the kid ain't here, we've got to find him and shut his mouth."

Tom Mohawk was still shaking his head as he mounted and started after Sanders' horse. "Tried to kill me, damn his ornery hide. Why did he do it?"

"He was a woman," Weston said contemptuously. "He had skimmed milk in his veins."

A few minutes later they started down the road, Weston leading Sanders' horse, his body draped across the saddle. Tom Mohawk said, "You're wrong, Cole. Took guts to pull a gun on me. I just can't figure why he done it."

Joe grinned at Tom and Tom grinned back. Now Bridlebit range was theirs for the taking.

Chapter 12

BARNEY DE LONG HAD NEVER SEEN THE RESULTS OF A LYNCH-ing until he drove around the store building and saw Cronin's body dangling from the cottonwood limb. He pulled up, staring in horror. He said hoarsely, "My God, Regan, that's terrible!"

"It's not pretty," Price said. "Stay there. I want to look around before we cut the body down."

De Long kept staring at Cronin's body as if hypnotized by it. He asked, "Who'd do a thing like that?"

Price had stepped out of the saddle. Now he looked at De Long, wondering if the man was serious. He said, "You can guess as good as I can."

He turned his back to De Long, walking carefully over the wet ground. The river had overflowed here not long before, leaving a coating of mud on the grass, so the sign was easy to read. Four horses, all right, just as Jean Potter had said. Two men had left boot prints under the tree. Another man had ridden up close, probably the one who had quirted the horse out from under Cronin. Price was able to follow the boot tracks of the two men back to their horses.

One thing was puzzling. From the tracks one of the men seemed to have remained out of the activity completely. He must, Price decided, have sat his saddle thirty yards or so from the tree; then, when it was over, he had swung toward the road and ridden downstream. The others had followed. Or preceded him. Price had no way of knowing the order.

For a time he stood pondering this. He was curious about the identity of the man who had taken no part in the hanging. Cole Weston, maybe, who hadn't wanted to dirty his hands with it. Price shook his head. No, that wasn't like him. He'd want to have a part of it, as much as he hated Walt Cronin.

Another point bothered Price. Why had all four of them ridden downstream? Only Red Sanders' Bridlebit lay in that direction. Maybe they hadn't wanted to run into anybody between Saddle Rock and the store. Price shrugged, deciding it wasn't important.

He had found nothing that helped him identify the four men, so it was more imperative than ever that he find the Jarvis boy. If the kid had ridden off, Price's job would be like hunting the proverbial needle in the haystack. More than that, there was a good chance the lynchers would run into him. But it seemed more natural for the boy to hide somewhere along the Yellow Cat and come back in a day or two as Sam Potter had told him to do. At least Price thought it was that way.

The kid would be safer if he hid out near the settlers than if he struck out across the open range where he was likely to be seen by a cowboy and brought in to one of the three ranches. The question, then, was whether Weston and the others knew the boy was a witness to the hanging. If they didn't know, they'd guess, Price decided, once they realized the kid was on the run.

"You gonna stand there all day, Regan?" De Long demanded.

"Reckon I've stood here long enough, Barney," Price answered, and motioned for the liveryman to drive the wagon under the limb that held the body.

When the wagon stopped, Price stepped up into the bed and, taking out his pocket knife, slashed at the rope with his right hand, easing the body down into the wagon when the last strand parted. He covered Cronin with the canvas De Long had thrown into the wagon before he'd left town, then vaulted over the side to the ground.

"Don't start back yet, Barney," Price said. "Drive to the front of the store and tie the team. We may find Rose around here somewhere."

De Long grumbled something about not wanting to find the woman if he could help it, but he obeyed. Price stepped into the saddle and followed the wagon. He dismounted, and tied his roan beside the team.

"Let's take a look in her cabin," he said.

"Rose won't make no witness if you do find her," De Long grumbled.

"Not if the trial was held in Saddle Rock," Price agreed, "but it won't be."

The cabin was empty, as Price had been reasonably certain it would be. The interior looked just about as he had expected. Dirty dishes were on the table. A greasy frying pan was on the back of the stove. The floor apparently hadn't been swept for a week. The bed covers had been thrown back and Rose's clothes were on the floor.

De Long stood in the doorway, his mouth curled in distaste. "She sure was a dirty bitch," he said. "Looks like she pulled out in a hurry. What do you suppose they done with her?"

"Hard to tell," Price said.

He turned and walked out, De Long stepping from the doorway. They crossed the road to the store, Price convinced they wouldn't find the woman alive. He wouldn't have been surprised if they'd strung her up alongside Cronin, but maybe even Weston couldn't stomach lynching a woman.

"They sure as hell got rid of her," De Long said. "Maybe they knocked her in the head and threw her into the river. Them Mohawks . . ."

He stopped, plainly regretting he'd said that much. Price nodded at him. "Might just as well say it right out, Barney. You know who did this as well as I do, and you know Barry Madden is as thick with them as five peas in a pod. Where are you and everybody else in town going to stand when this comes out into the open?"

"I don't know nothing 'bout it," De Long mumbled. "I just wish I'd stayed in town and let you sing when you told me to come out here."

Price let it drop, knowing he'd given De Long something to think about. By sundown everybody in town would be thinking the same thing, but Price couldn't count on help from any of them, not as long as Barry Madden continued to back Cole Weston.

Price went into the store, De Long lingering in the doorway. Here he found evidence of a struggle and a rifle on the floor at the base of the counter. Walt Cronin had been a tough nut, just as Price had told him the day before, but not tough enough to buck the four men who had come after him. He wondered what had prompted Cronin to come here and open up a store and back the settlers when he knew what he was up against. But whatever his motives were, he'd made a bad mistake, foolishly overestimating his capacity to resist. So he'd bet his blue chips and he'd lost, not even able to take Cole Weston with him.

Going into the storeroom, Price was surprised at how thin the light was with the back door closed. Again he realized it could have happened exactly as Jean Potter had said, the kid hiding in a dark corner and Red Sanders walking past him without seeing him.

Price stepped through the back door, noticing the corner made by the leanto room where the boy had left his team and wagon. Well, there was nothing more he could do. He'd send De Long back to town with the body and then he'd ride up the Yellow Cat, hoping he would find the boy.

He heard something from the riverbank. Limbs breaking, maybe. He yanked his gun from holster, calling, "De

Long!" It could be the kid, although this was the last place where he expected to find him.

He ran toward the river, gaze running up and down the screen of willows. De Long appeared in the back door of the store, holding back as if reluctant to give any help. Price yelled above the sound of the river, "Somebody's hiding along here. Come on." Slowly De Long moved toward him. Exasperated, Price shouted, "Damn it, get a move on! You head downstream."

A moment later De Long called, "I found her. It's Rose."

Price holstered his gun and ran to where the man stood, forefinger pointing into the willows. He saw her, then, as motionless as if she were frozen, facing him as she squatted precariously on the bank of the stream, both hands holding to the base of two willows. She looked at him, blinking. She was wearing nothing but her nightgown, and it had been ripped by the brush in half a dozen places so it did little to hide her nakedness.

"Come out of there, Rose," Price ordered. "We're not going to hurt you."

Still she squatted there, bare feet in the mud, staring at him with blank eyes as if she had never seen him before. He started to reach for her arm and then dropped his hand, realizing that if she relaxed her hold on the willows she'd fall into the river and drown. It was deep and swift here close to the bank, and ice-cold, coming as it did right from the snow banks of the Singing Wind Range.

He turned his head to De Long. "Move downstream a little. If she falls, maybe you can grab her." He looked at Rose again, edging forward. "I'm Price Regan, the deputy. You remember me, Rose. I'm here to get the men who killed Walt Cronin."

"Walt Cronin." She repeated the name as if it stirred her memory.

He eased forward again, right hand close to her left arm. "Come on, Rose. Let's go get dressed. Nobody's going to hurt you. We're here to help you."

His words were beginning to get through to her. Then

terror was in her again and she screamed, "They're going to kill me! You're going to give me to them!"

He grabbed her wrist just in time. She let go and slid toward the water. Now, with her right arm free, she was swung completely around, the current tugging hard at her body. "Give me a hand, De Long!" Price shouted. "Hurry up!"

Price had both hands on her wrist, muscles standing out in hard knots as he fought the river, and for a terrible moment he thought the current was going to tear her from his grip. Then De Long was stooping beside Price, helping him, and together they pulled her out of the water and through the mud between the willows to dry ground.

They got her feet under her, but she lacked the will or the strength to stand. They practically carried her around the store to her cabin. Only her head and arms had stayed out of the water, and she was shaking violently from fear or the chill from being in the cold water, or both.

She didn't resist. She didn't try to talk. She just went along, her head wobbling from one side to the other, and when they laid her on the bed, she was little more than an inert mass of flesh, mud smeared from her breasts down her stomach and legs to her feet.

"Get into the store and fetch a bottle of whisky," Price said. "We've got to bring her out of this."

De Long obeyed. Price pumped a pan of water at the sink in the corner of the room and, grabbing a towel from a nail behind the stove, dipped one end into the water and washed her face and arms and feet.

"Can you get up and dress, Rose?" Price asked. "You're soaking wet. We've got to get that nightgown off of you."

"You won't let them have me?" she asked, her eyes on him in that expressionless dead-fish stare that frightened him.

He wondered if she ever would come out of it. He said,

"You're safe, Rose. I won't let them have you. Can you tell me who it was?"

"Don't let them get me," she begged. "Please! Don't let them get me."

No use to question her now. He said, "I won't let them get you, Rose. You're safe."

De Long came in with the whisky and would have left if Price hadn't said, "Stay here, Barney. If she says anything, I want you to hear it."

"What'll my wife say?" De Long muttered. "Ain't she a mess?"

Price slid an arm under her head and, lifting it, put the bottle to her lips and tilted it. She took a long drink and choked, but it did something for her. He gave her another drink and let her head drop back to the pillow.

For a long time she stared at him, then she said, "You're Regan, ain't you?"

"That's right." He took her hand that was nearest to him. "You're safe now. You're all right."

"Walt could have licked you."

"Maybe, but that's past. What we want to do is to get the men who killed him."

For a moment he thought he'd made a mistake mentioning Cronin's death. She raised up, a crazy violence coming into her eyes. Then she dropped back, shivering. "Yeah, we've gotta get them dirty bastards."

"You feel like getting dressed yet?" he asked.

"Don't make no difference."

"Yes, it makes a lot of difference. I'm going to send you to town and you can take the stage to Rawlins in the morning. You'll be safe there."

She rubbed her face with both hands. "Rawlins? I'd be safe there, wouldn't I? Walt's dead, ain't he?"

"Yes. Now will you get dressed?"

"All right," she said listlessly.

She got up, swaying a moment before the dizziness left her. She slipped out of the muddy nightgown. Price and De Long turned to the door. She said, in the same listless tone, "Don't make no difference. Better men than you have seen me naked." She picked up the towel and wiped the mud off the front of her body. "Better men than you are gonna see me naked, too. I'm going to Rawlins."

She finished dressing and sat down in front of the mirror that hung on the wall and began to brush her hair. De Long grimaced. He said, in a low tone, "Ain't she a mess? What'll my wife say when I tell her about this?"

"Don't tell her."

"Aw, she'll get it out of me."

"Listen, Barney. You take Rose to the hotel as soon as you get to town and see she gets a room. I can't go back to town now, but I'll be there tonight. I don't want her running around the streets and I don't want anybody getting into her room and killing her."

"You don't think that would happen?" De Long demanded.

"Anything can happen now. It'd be best if you got somebody to stay with her. Laura, maybe."

"Barry wouldn't stand for it."

"No, I guess he wouldn't. Well, Jean Potter then. And you tell Barry that Cole Weston is in a pile of trouble, and Barry's going to be in the same trouble if he don't make a quick move."

"I'll tell him, but he won't like it," De Long said. "Aw, this is a mess."

Price walked to where Rose sat in front of the mirror. He said, "Can you tell me what happened?"

She gave him a sidelong glance, her eyes filled with cunning. "Did something happen?"

"Who killed Walt?"

"I don't remember."

He turned away, disgusted and angry. De Long had heard her, and he asked, "What's the matter with her now?"

"She's playing cute," Price said.

"I'm going to Rawlins," Rose said. "I'm going to pack a suitcase and I'm never coming back."

Price left the cabin, jerking his head at De Long. When they reached the wagon, Price said, "Don't let her get away from you on the way to town. She's as crazy as if she'd been eating locoweed."

De Long groaned. "What'll my wife say, with that woman riding beside me all the way to town?"

"Be careful she don't get you into the brush," Price said, and went into the store.

Cronin had no safe, but in his leanto room Price found a heavy oak chest with a padlock on it. He got an ax and smashed it open, and was surprised at the amount of money he found, both gold and greenbacks. He didn't stop to count it, but it must have been several thousand dollars. He dropped it into a canvas sack that he found in the chest and pulled the drawstrings tight.

When he returned to the wagon, he saw that Rose had dropped her suitcase on top of Cronin's body in the bed and had climbed to the seat. She was wearing a cartwheel hat with a gigantic red plume bending back over the brim. Price restrained a grin. Barney De Long might have trouble with his wife at that.

"Soon as you get to town, go to the hotel and stay there. I'll see you tonight. You understand? Don't leave your room."

"I understand. I won't leave."

De Long stepped up to the seat and took the lines. Price nodded at him as he drove away, looking completely uncomfortable. Price did grin as he turned toward his horse. He wondered what Mrs. De Long would say.

Chapter 13

PRICE STOPPED AT THE EVANS PLACE ON HIS WAY UP THE
Yellow Cat. He didn't really expect to learn anything
from Frank Evans, but he was the closest settler to the
store, so there was a slim chance he had seen or heard
something that would help build a case against Cole
Weston and his friends.

Knowing that they had murdered Walt Cronin and
proving it in court were two different things. It would
take an iron-clad case to convict them, even if the trial
was held in the county seat. They had money and
influence, and they'd hire the best lawyers in the state.

Even if Price had Bruce Jarvis to testify, he wouldn't
have an iron-clad case, judging from what Jean had told
him. As yet, he had learned nothing from Rose, and he
wasn't sure he would, or that her testimony would be of
any help if she had anything to say.

He dismounted and knocked on Evan's door. When
there was no answer, he went in. The cabin was empty.
He went out, closing the door, vaguely alarmed because
he had a capacity for sensing when things were wrong.

Evans should have made an appearance if he was here. Of course, he might have gone to the Potters or one of the other neighbors. He might have heard about Cronin and lit a shuck out of the country. They'd all be on their way in a day or two, Price thought. There wasn't a fighting man in the Yellow Cat bunch, and with Cronin dead they wouldn't even try to resist.

He crossed the yard to the shed and stopped in the doorway, shocked by what he saw. Red Sanders lay face down in the barn litter. Frank Evans was about twenty feet from him at the far end of the shed. A .44 Colt lay between, closer to Evans than to Sanders. Both were dead, and apparently had been for several hours.

Carefully Price walked inside, keeping close to the wall, and spent some time examining the scene. The fact that there was only one gun puzzled him. Whose was it, and had it killed both men? Those were questions he couldn't answer. There was, he thought, the possibility they had wrestled over the gun, one had been shot, and then he had succeeded in taking the Colt from the other man and had shot him.

A possibility, but a slim one, both men hit as hard as they had been. Sanders must have died at once, Evans might have lived a few minutes. The gun, Price was sure, belonged to Sanders. His holster was empty. It was doubtful that Evans ever owned a six-shooter.

Returning to the yard, Price examined it for tracks, but the ground was hard and he found nothing conclusive. Horses had been here this morning, but that proved nothing. He mounted his roan and turned up the creek toward the Potter place, puzzled by the fact that of the four men who had hanged Cronin, Red Sanders was the one who was killed. Sanders would be the last man to shoot Frank Evans, especially if the man didn't have a gun.

One other possibility occurred to Price. Sanders might have shot Evans and one of the other settlers had been there, perhaps unknown to Sanders, and he had cut

Sanders down and fled. The gun might have dropped from Sanders' hand as he fell. But this theory didn't hold water simply because Price knew the caliber of the people who lived on the Yellow Cat, and he didn't believe any of them were capable of shooting Sanders. He was sure, too, that Sanders would not have shot Evans down in cold blood.

Then another question occurred to Price. Why had Sanders been here in the first place? Now the picture was completely muddied and he gave up. It was natural that the men who had hanged Cronin would get away from the scene of the hanging as fast as they could.

When he reached the Potter farm, he was surprised again. Fifty people or more were gathered in the yard. As his eyes ran over the group, it seemed to him that everybody who lived on the Yellow Cat was here. Suddenly he realized that neither Sam nor Lizzie Potter was in the group.

He stepped down, the settlers falling back before him, eyeing him with the same hostility he always felt when he met any of these people. But there was something else, too. They weren't talking. They weren't moving around. They acted as if they were under some kind of spell. Even the children, normally noisy and filled with perpetual motion, stood staring at him.

Finally George Farnum said, "I reckon you brought us the word, but there don't need to be no more killing. Give us the rest of the day to load up and we'll be moving out in the morning. That's all we're asking. Just the rest of the day."

They were scared. He saw that now. But it was more than just fear. They were completely terrorized. He stared at the men who had moved out to stand in front of their women and children. Farnum. Ripley. Wagner. Bailey. Others whose names he didn't know.

"I didn't bring you any word," Price said. "Maybe you're afraid of me because you've been stealing. If you have, you've got a right to be, but if it's because Cronin's been telling you I'm a hired gun for the cowmen, you can quit being scared. I don't belong to the cowmen and I never have. I'm here to find some proof about who lynched Cronin.

They showed they didn't believe him. He asked, "Which killing did you mean, Farnum? Cronin's or Evans'?"

"Evans?" Farnum asked incredulously. "You mean Frank's dead?"

"You didn't know?"

"How would we know?" Farnum said. "We didn't get no farther than right here. I reckon we didn't even miss Frank." He swore with the anguish of a man who had been completely whipped by the injustice of life. He waved a big hand toward the house. "You wanted to know what killing. Them! We found 'em when we came. We always have dinner here on a Sunday if the weather ain't too bad, and some preaching. Me'n' my girls got here first. We found 'em yonder." He motioned again. "Lizzie had her head propped up on the first step of the porch. Sam, he was over here flat on the ground. We moved 'em into the shade and covered 'em with quilts."

The crowd parted in front of Price. For the first time he saw the bodies, the feet sticking out from under the quilts. He moved to them and turning the quilts back, took one quick look at Sam's and Lizzie's faces, then covered them again and walked away. He had known Weston and his friends would go as far as murdering a woman if they thought it necessary. Now he had seen the proof of it. He knew that Rose, too, would have been killed if she hadn't hidden in the brush along the river.

"We ain't found hide nor hair of Jean or Bruce," Farnum said. "You reckon they . . ."

"Jean's in town and she's safe," Price said. "I'm going to keep her there. I won't let her come to the funeral. Maybe I won't tell her about her folks yet."

"Bruce. What happened to him?" It was a slender, thin-faced girl standing behind Farnum. She had been crying, and now her hands were clenched at her sides, her body so tense she could hardly breathe.

"That's my youngest," Farnum said. "She's Bruce's girl."

"I don't know where Bruce is," Price said. "I'm hunting him. He was in the store when Cronin was strung up. He's the key witness to this whole thing. If any of you have seen him—"

The girl cried out and whirled and ran toward the barn. "Hey," Price called. "Wait!" But she didn't wait. He turned to Farnum. "What's her name?"

"Susie. She's worried about the boy . . ."

"I've got to talk to her," Price said, and ran after the girl.

She reached the barn ahead of him and tried to shut the door and keep him out, but he pushed the door back and caught her by the hands. "Susie. Listen to me. You've got to help."

A big, coarse-featured girl ran up and began pounding Price on the back. "You quit bothering Susie. I'm her sister Dora. The kid's gone. Let him go. He wasn't no good for Susie anyhow."

Price let go of Susie's hands and wheeled on Dora. "Get out of here. Farnum! Pull this one off my back or I'll twist her neck."

Dora backed off as Farnum came up. "I'm just trying to help Susie . . ."

"Let him alone," her father said heavily. "I don't know what he's doing, but maybe he does."

Price turned to Susie, who had fled to the far side of the barn and cowered against the wall. He walked slowly toward her, saying, "Susie, I'm not going to hurt you. I want to help you."

She was crying steadily, and several minutes passed before she quieted down enough for him to talk to her. When she was finally able to listen, he said, "You love Bruce, don't you?"

"Yes," she whispered, rubbing an arm across her eyes.

"The Potters never treated him good and he was going to run away tonight. He was going to get a job and maybe he'd have let me know where he was. Now they'll catch him and kill him just like they done with Cronin and the Potters and—and Frank Evans."

"Maybe not," Price said. "He's too smart to just strike off across the grass and take a chance on running into some cowboy. I've got a notion he's hiding here along the Yellow Cat. There's lots of brush and a dozen side canyons where he could hide for a week and not be found. Before he left, Sam told him to hide out a day or two and come back. We've got to count on him doing that."

"Then maybe I'll see him," Susie said. "He said he'd see me before he left."

"That's what I was getting at," Price said. Farnum, he saw, had come into the barn and was standing behind him. "Susie, if Bruce comes to see you, I want you to tell him something. It's important. It's so important that maybe it'll save his life and the lives of all of you. Will you tell him?"

She nodded eagerly. "I'll tell him, Mr. Regan."

"Tell him to come to town and see me. I'll protect him. I want him to tell me everything he saw. When I arrest Cole Weston and the Mohawk boys, I want him to testify at their trial. Will you tell him that?"

The eagerness went out of her. "But that's dangerous, Mr. Regan. If they know he's going to testify . . ."

"Listen, Susie. Everything about this business is dangerous. If he keeps running, they're bound to find him. When they do, they'll kill him. The way I've got it sized up, they shot the Potters so they couldn't tell what they knew. If I don't keep Jean in town, they'll kill her. Hard to tell whether they know Bruce was the one in the store or not, but they must know it was one of the Potters or they wouldn't have come here. This is the only way, Susie. Don't you see that?"

"I see," she whispered. "I'll tell him, Mr. Regan."

"Good." He patted her on the shoulder and walked out, nodding for Farnum to come with him. When they were outside, he said, "Jean says that Potter told Bruce to come back after he hid out a day or two. He won't know what happened to Potter, so chances are he'll show up tonight or tomorrow night. I want you to stay here and grab him if he comes. Between you and Susie maybe we'll get him."

"No." Farnum shook his head. "I ain't gonna hang around here and have that bunch ride in and do me like they done Sam. No, sir."

Price stopped and took Farnum by the arm. He said, "Listen, friend. You're in trouble. All of you, unless Weston hangs. I aim to see that he does, but I've got to have that boy for a witness."

Farnum scratched the toe of his shoe back and forth in the dirt, his eyes on the ground. "You ain't man enough to go after Weston and take him."

"I'm man enough to try," Price said sharply. "That's all I'm asking of you."

Farnum kept on scratching his toe in the dirt. "I dunno," he said.

Angry now, Price said, "You chuckle-headed idiot, don't you see that if they want to kill you they'll do it whether you're here or at your own place? If you stay or run, they'll get you if that's what they think they've got to do. Your only chance is for me to get hold of that boy and send Weston where he belongs."

Farnum looked up. "How are you gonna ride into the Rocking C and fetch old Weston out? It'd take an army to do it."

"I don't know how, but I will," Price said. "I've never failed to bring a man in that I went after. But that's not the point. Right now I've got to have that boy."

Farnum took a long breath. "All right, Regan. I'll stay here."

Price nodded curtly and strode across the yard where the rest of them stood huddled in a tight little group.

Price said, "You folks go ahead with the burying. Like I told you, I'm keeping Jean in town. Remember that Bruce Jarvis is the key to what happens to you and to Weston and everybody else on this range. If Weston can commit murder and get away scot free, there will never be any law or peace in this country."

They stared at the ground, silent, still scared. He went on, "I'm coming back in the morning to look for Bruce. If you haven't got him, I'll expect you men to help me look for him."

He wheeled to his horse and mounted and rode back down the creek. They wouldn't help, he thought. He doubted if Farnum would keep his promise and stay at the Potter place tonight. Even if Susie kept her promise and told Bruce to come in, he didn't think the boy would do it.

Farnum was right about needing an army to take Weston. He, Price Regan, was the law, but the star he carried didn't make his hide tough enough to deflect a bullet.

Again that terrible feeling of being entirely alone descended upon him. He wondered what Sheriff Ralph Carew would do in a situation like this.

Chapter 14

A SHORT DISTANCE BELOW FRANK EVAN'S FARM THE SIDES OF the Yellow Cat were less precipitous than they were upstream. As soon as the climb was not too difficult, Price turned to his left and, by taking a switchback course, was able to reach the top. From this point he could see the Elk River Valley for miles. He thought again, as he had so many times in the past, that regardless of what Cole Weston did now, it would not be many years until the settler tide moved across the Singing Wind Range and filled the valley from one end to the other.

Across the river Rocking C range stretched south to the horizon, as good a stock country as Price had ever seen. Weston should be satisfied with it and not play dog in the manger with the fertile valley land that could be farmed. But from his own experience Price knew that a cowman of Weston's stripe was never satisfied.

The east half of Tremaine County was as different from this side as day from night. Hundreds of prosperous farms were scattered around the county seat. A railroad and telegraph line had been built in from Denver. Now there was even talk of telephones.

The one great fact that overshadowed everything else in Price's thinking was that twenty years ago, when Ralph Carew had first taken the sheriff's star, that end of the county was exactly like Elk River Valley was now. There had been Cole Westons on that range, too, but the pressure of organized society had forced them out of existence. That pressure was exemplified in Ralph Carew. Here, on Elk River, Carew's counterpart was Price Regan. A hell of a position for a man to be in, he thought sourly, and remembered George Farnum saying that it would take an army to go into the Rocking C and come out with Cole Weston.

Price took his glasses from the case, for the moment trying to forget how impossible his position was. He studied the country to the south, picking up half a dozen riders scattered over the hills. Looking westward down the valley, he spotted two more.

Broken Ring range to the north was much like Rocking C to the south, stretching twenty miles to a high range of hills that heaved up against the sky and marked the north boundary of Broken Ring. After several minutes' scrutiny, Price discovered four riders who were on the move. Across the Yellow Cat on Bridlebit grass he could not see a single man.

Price slipped the glasses back into the case and buckled the lid down, thinking about this. Red Sanders was dead, so for the moment no one on Bridlebit was giving orders. Price turned his horse toward the river, and followed the rim of the Yellow Cat until it was no longer a rim, but a gentle slope. A few minutes later he reached the county road some distance upstream from Cronin's store and turned toward town.

He wondered what would happen to Bridlebit, now that Sanders was dead. The Mohawk boys were as greedy and ambitious as Weston. Maybe they would devour it, buying it from Sanders' widow for a song, or simply seizing and holding it by force.

No, Weston would not permit it, Price thought. He would want to hold Broken Ring to its present size. Perhaps he would go to Mrs. Sanders' aid, sending her a foreman and additional riders who would give Bridlebit the strength it needed to fight off the Mohawks. That would be like Weston, going to any length to retain his present preeminent position.

Price's thoughts returned to what he had seen from the rim above the Yellow Cat, a dozen or more riders, moving in a zigzag, apparently aimless, fashion. Now it was late afternoon, and Weston and the Mohawk boys had had time to return to their headquarters ranches after the hanging. There seemed to be only one explanation. They had ordered their men to search for Bruce Jarvis. If they found him, Price's chance of getting a conviction for the murder of Walt Cronin stood exactly at zero.

When Price reached the bridge that crossed Elk River and led to the Rocking C, he came to a decision. Turning across the bridge, he rode toward Weston's ranch that lay half a mile to the south at the base of the rise that lifted from the rich meadowland along the river.

This was a calculated gamble, Price knowing exactly the chance he was taking. He kept thinking of Farnum's words, that it would take an army to arrest Cole Weston. He didn't have an army and he couldn't get one. Raising a posse to go after Weston was an absurdity that was not worthy of consideration. Granting that it became possible, made so by Barry Madden changing position, it would lead to a bloody battle that could still end in failure.

On the other hand, going in alone might accomplish something, even if it amounted only to an act of defiance. He felt reasonably certain that Weston wouldn't kill him at this point. The man was coldly logical, and common sense dictated that the proper approach was to prevent Price from obtaining the evidence that would lead to a trial and conviction. Weston would certainly not be above murdering a deputy, but it would be the last resort.

Price held his horse down to a walk, his gun riding easily in leather, his right hand holding the reins, his left at his side. Cole Weston was the kind of man who admired and feared tough, cold courage above all other qualities, and that was what it took to ride into Rocking C alone as Price was doing now. If Price knew his man, he could count on this visit making Weston overly cautious. That, in the end, could well lead to his defeat.

Price followed the lane formed by parallel fences that enclosed the hay fields between the buildings and the river. Weston, Price remembered, had a wife but no children. Mrs. Weston seldom came to town. Price had seen her only twice, a slender, gray-haired woman completely dominated by her husband. That, of course, was in line with Cole Weston's nature. He wouldn't stand for any other kind of woman sharing his life.

The appearance of the ranch bore out this same quality in Weston. It was strictly a man's ranch, built for efficiency without the slightest hint that a woman lived here. No grass in front of the sprawling stone house, no flowers, not even a white lace curtain at any of the windows. Just the red drapes in the front room. The only break in the harsh monotony was a single cottonwood tree that shaded the hitch rail in front of the house, planted there, perhaps, when Weston had pioneered this ranch a generation ago.

When Price reined up under the cottonwood, he saw that two men were watching him from one of the corrals, both strangers. Three riders were coming down the ridge behind the buildings.

Now, a moment after Price pulled his horse to a stop, Pete Nance came out of the bunkhouse and moved toward him in slow, deliberate steps.

Price sat his saddle, thinking Weston would come out of the house, but he didn't. The two men who had been in front of the corral disappeared. Except for Nance, Price seemed to be completely ignored.

The gunman stopped twenty feet from Price in the back of the patch of shade, the sun to his back. He wasn't wearing his Stetson or his spurs. He looked as if he had just shaved, and, as usual, he was wearing both guns.

"What do you want, Regan?" Nance asked.

"I'm here to see Weston," Price said.

Nance smiled briefly. With easy disdain, he lifted paper and tobacco from his shirt pocket and rolled a smoke, the hot slanting sunlight pressing upon his back. He sealed the cigarette and slipped it into his mouth, fished around in his pocket for a match, thumbed it to life and touched the flame to the cigarette. He dropped the charred match into the dust, and then, with the cigarette hanging from his lower lip, he said, "Mr. Weston don't want to see you. Not today."

Price understood the game. This was deliberate provocation that didn't seem to be provocation at all. If Price let his temper get away from him and made a foolish move, Nance would kill him and the law wouldn't touch him, if there was any law left to touch him.

So Price played it out, holding a tight rein to his temper. The part that infuriated him was the fact that when you bucked a man like Cole Weston, you always had someone of Pete Nance's caliber between you and your real enemy. Curly Blue, too, if he were here.

The silence ran on for a time, Price leaning forward and placing both hands on the saddle horn. He said, "I want to see Weston whether he wants to see me or not."

Again the silence ribboned out, Nance keeping his gaze on Price, hands at his sides, the cigarette on his lip. Finally he said, "I reckon you didn't hear, Regan. Weston don't want to see you today."

Price's right hand dropped to his side so it was within inches of the butt of his gun, his left still on the saddle horn. This, again, was a calculated gamble, for Price had no way of knowing how far Nance was prepared to go, or what his orders had been, but he didn't think Weston wanted a showdown here. He would probably prefer a killing in town where everyone could see it was a fair fight.

"I heard you," Price said, "but maybe you didn't hear me. You want to call Weston, or do I get off my horse and go to the door?"

Slowly Nance's left hand lifted to his mouth, took the cigarette from his lip and dropped it to the ground. He placed the toe of his right foot on it and rubbed it out. All the time his gaze was pinned on Price's face, the faintly amused expression lingering there.

"I'll call him," he said, and without turning toward the house, raised his voice to shout, "Boss, this hairpin wants to see you."

A moment later Weston stalked out of the house, slamming the screen shut, and strode across the yard. He was dusty, unshaven and cranky, his long hair falling across his face. He brushed it back, glaring at Price.

"I was just about to sit down to supper with my wife, Regan," Weston said. "What do you want?"

One glance told Price the call was worth while. Weston was worried, worried so much he couldn't hide it. His plans for the day had not gone to please him. Price's visit plainly added to that worry, so that talk called for caution.

"Red Sanders was shot and killed today," Price said. "I thought you'd want to know."

Weston was jolted, whether by the news or because Price had brought the information was something Price couldn't determine.

"Who done it?" Weston demanded.

"I don't know," Price answered. "I thought you might have a notion."

"Maybe I do," Weston said. "Where'd you find him?"

"In Frank Evans's shed. Evans was dead, too."

"Hell, it's plain enough. They shot each other. I knew what that Yellow Cat bunch would do if you let 'em stay."

"I don't think it was that way," Price said. "There was

just one gun on the ground between them."

"That don't prove nothing. Chances are they fought over the gun and one of 'em got plugged. Then he grabbed the gun and drilled the one who shot him."

So that was the way it was supposed to look. Price nodded. "Maybe. Only it must have been Sanders' gun because his holster was empty. Chances are Evans didn't own a six-shooter. They were both hit hard. Sanders died quick. Evans might have lived a few minutes."

Weston shrugged, his glance flicking to Pete Nance and returning to Price. "For a deputy who's supposed to be able to read signs, you're blinder'n a bat. I can tell you what happened. Red went up the Yellow Cat to look into the stealing he's been having. He quarreled with Evans and shot him, and then one of them bastardly nesters who was hiding there drilled him. You'd better get back up the Yellow Cat and arrest the one that done it."

"I'm working on it," Price said. "I thought you could send a man after the body and take it home. And tell Mrs. Sanders, seeing as you were a friend of Red's."

"Sure, I'll take care of it."

Weston turned toward the house. Price said, "One more thing, Cole. I'm looking for Bruce Jarvis. If you find him, fetch him to me. Don't let anything happen to him."

Weston whirled as if a tightly wound spring had been released inside him. "Who's Bruce Jarvis?"

Once more Price had taken a calculated gamble. Now it was touch and go. "He's the kid who worked for the Potters," Price said. "He left home, stealing their saddle horse. I want him and the horse."

The relief that flowed across Weston's face was painful. "Not much chance I'll see him," Weston said, "but if I do I'll send him in to you."

"Thanks, Cole," Price said, and, touching up his horse, rode away.

Prickles played along his spine until he reached the bridge. He didn't think he'd be shot in the back, but

Weston was jumpy, so jumpy that anything could happen. Reaching the county road, Price turned toward town.

Strange, he thought grimly, that in this talk with Weston nothing had been said of Cronin's hanging or the murder of Sam and Lizzie Potter. He had a strong feeling that if he had mentioned either, he would not have left the Rocking C alive.

Still, he had no way of knowing what went on inside Cole Weston's head, now that he had gone this far. But one thing was sure. Weston had to remove a deputy he could not control, and he knew beyond any doubt by this time that he could not control Price Regan. In the morning Pete Nance would probably be in town looking for him.

Chapter 15

PRICE WAS DEAD TIRED WHEN HE REACHED TOWN, WORN DOWN to a nubbin both physically and emotionally. He put his horse away in the livery stable, not seeing Barney De Long. The night man had come on. Probably Barney was home listening to his wife, Price thought as he stepped into Grandma Spivey's Café for supper.

"Get me the quickest meal you can," he said.

"I can slice you some cold roast," she said, "and I've got beans and coffee on the stove. You're traveling late, Marshal. I was fixing to lock up for the night."

"That's fine," he said. "Fetch me some coffee now."

She brought him a cup of coffee, scalding hot, and he stirred it with a spoon. What a terrible, bloody Sunday it had been! Funny, he thought, how the very things a man fears actually come to pass, and the good things he wants are forbidden to him.

He had been afraid this trouble with Cronin would blow up before he had a chance to see Ralph Carew. He had been equally afraid he wouldn't live long enough to marry Laura. Right now it looked like a safe bet that he didn't have more than forty-eight hours left, if he found

Bruce Jarvis and could persuade the boy to testify in court.

Grandma Spivey brought his meal, went back to the kitchen and returned with a wide slab of dried apple pie. She was a big woman who puffed and sweated profusely through the hot summer weather. She had the only eating place in town, and kept it open every day in the week and on Sunday as soon as she could get here from church.

She had a heart as big as a washtub. She never made much money because she was overgenerous with credit, giving meals to every deadbeat who came in. She'd work from sunup until after sundown in the café, and then sit up all night with anyone who was sick.

But she was in love with holy virtue, too, and now she folded her fat arms over her pillow-like bosom and asked ominously, "When's that woman you've got over there in the hotel going to leave town, Marshal?"

Price held his tongue for a moment, knowing he would gain nothing by saying what he wanted to say. It struck him that goodness ran in strange streaks, and Grandma Spivey was typical of the town. Good neighbors, good people, honest and righteous and law-abiding who would go along with just about anything Barry Madden said. Walt Cronin's hanging wouldn't bother them too much. They'd be horrified by the news of the Potters' murder, but even if they knew the facts they'd find some excuse for Cole Weston. On the other hand, Rose's presence in town was one thing they could not tolerate.

"Grandma," Price said when his temper was under control, "you just stay away from Rose and you won't get what she's got."

It took a moment for the implication of Price's words to get through to Grandma Spivey. When it did, she glared at him, as insulted as if he had actually questioned her virtue. Without a word, she turned and tramped back into the kitchen and stayed there until he finished, tossed a coin on the counter, and left.

He wanted to go to bed, but there was too much to do.

He had to tell Jean Potter what had happened. He had put it off as long as he could, for he knew it would be one of the hardest things he'd ever been forced to do.

When he rang the Madden doorbell, it occurred to him that he was living in a strange cycle of recurring events. This was the third time in a little over twenty-four hours that he'd stood here expecting Barry Madden to open the door and tell him he wasn't welcome.

But it was Laura who opened the door to him. For just a moment she peered into the darkness, the bracket lamp on the wall throwing her shadow past him across the porch, then she saw who it was and cried, "Price!" She fled into his arms and he held her for a moment, feeling that he wasn't alone as long as he had her love.

She drew his face down and kissed him, then she said, "We've been crazy with worry. Did you find Bruce?"

"No, but I've got to see Jean. Is she here?"

"Of course she's here. I wouldn't let her go anywhere. Barney De Long came and said maybe she ought to go stay with that Rose person, but I wouldn't let her." She pulled Price into the hall where she could see him, her eyes searching his face. Then she said, "I'm worried about Daddy almost as much as I am about you. What's going to happen to him?"

"I don't know," Price said, his voice cranky in spite of himself. "He's picked his side."

She shivered as if she were cold, although the hall still held the stagnant heat of the day. She said, "I've quarreled with him about Jean staying here. I told him that if she left, I'd leave, too. He's nervous, Price. I've never seen him like this. I think he's afraid."

"He's got reason to be," Price said. "Let me talk to Jean."

Laura opened the door into the parlor. Jean stood looking expectantly at him, as if she had been waiting for him to come. She was wearing a clean, starched gingham dress. One of Laura's, Price thought. Laura had given her a pair of shoes, too. Once more he was impressed with the fact that she was an uncommonly pretty girl who deserved a far better life than she'd had out there on the Yellow Cat.

"Bruce?" Jean asked. "Did you find him?"

"No, but maybe some of your neighbors will. I'll try again in the morning." He motioned for her to sit down on the couch, wishing there was some way to make his task easier. He sat beside her, saying gently, "I've got bad news for you. Both of your parents were shot and killed today. I don't know who did it, but we'll find out."

She was very pale, but she didn't faint or become hysterical. She simply looked at him, her hands tightly fisted on her lap, then she said, "I've had a terrible feeling ever since I left home. I should have stayed."

He shook his head. "You couldn't have helped. You'd have been killed, too. Now I want you to stay here inside this house. I don't know if you're in danger or not, but we don't want to take any chances. I could put you in jail for your own safety, but I won't if you promise to stay here."

"I promise," she said automatically, as if she didn't really know what she was promising. "Mr. Regan, ever since I was a little girl I can't remember anything but moving around, being pushed by men like Cole Weston. Pa would get a job and lose it. Or he'd settle on a piece of land and have to get off. When you were out there, Ma said we'd never move again. If she was killed, she said her blood would soak into the ground. Maybe she knew what was going to happen."

Price rose. There was nothing more he could say or do. She was suffering the shock that sudden, terrible death brings to those who are left. The full sense of loss would come to her later.

She looked up at him. "Mr. Regan, I can't stay here. I'll have to go to the funeral."

"Your neighbors took care of it today."

She bowed her head and the tears came. Price moved to the door, and as he opened it he saw that Laura had sat down beside Jean and put her arm around the other girl.

Price stepped into the hall and closed the door. Then he saw that Barry Madden was waiting for him.

"Come back to the study, Price," Madden said. "I want to talk to you."

It was a peremptory order, given in the typical Madden manner. Price hesitated, noticing that Madden was nervous, as Laura had said. Price had never seen him this way before. He was pale, his pulse leaping in his temples, and even his hands were trembling.

"No use, Barry," Price said. "I can't do anything for you. You were the only one who could have helped yourself, and now it looks to me like you've waited too long."

"I don't expect you to do anything for me," Madden said harshly. "If you won't come back to the study, I'll tell you here. You're not marrying Laura. You're going to drop this whole business before it ruins me and all of us. Pack your things and leave town on the morning stage. I'll accept your resignation as marshal here and now."

"Do you really think I'll do that?" Price asked.

"You have no choice. You'll resign, or I'll call a meeting of the town council tomorrow and we'll fire you. Then I'll go to the county seat and have Ralph Carew recall you. Meanwhile, stay away from Laura."

"Barry, you can't be as stupid as you're talking. You're not like Cole Weston. You've got some decency in you."

Flushing, Madden said, "Good night," and turned away.

Price caught his arm. "In case you don't know what happened today, I'll tell you. Five people have been killed, and I'm convinced Cole Weston was responsible for every murder. That's your side, Barry, the side you picked."

He walked out, leaving Madden standing in the hall. He went to the hotel, wondering how much Madden had known, and how far he would go, now that he did know. There was still something he couldn't put his finger on, something that was behind Madden's blind following of

Cole Weston. It wasn't loyalty or devotion or friendship or any of the things that ordinarily prompt one man to back another.

Any way Price looked at this situation, it seemed a strange and unnatural alliance, with both men being impelled to dominate as they were. No, there was something else, and he was convinced that Laura didn't fully understand what it was.

When he stepped into the hotel lobby, the clerk said, "That woman Barney De Long brought in. She's in Room 10. Says she wants to see you."

Price nodded and climbing the stairs, knocked on Rose's door. She opened it, smiling coyly in the artificial way she had. "Come in, Deputy. I've been wondering what happened to you. They tell me the stage leaves early in the morning and I wanted to thank you for what you done for me."

"No need to thank me." He handed her the sack of money he had found in Cronin's store. "That was Cronin's. You might as well have it. I've been packing it around ever since I was out there. You were too worked up for me to give it to you when you left with Barney De Long."

"It ought to be mine. I deserve it more'n them damned thieving settlers do." She opened the sack and looked into it, her face taking on the expression of a greedy child, then she glanced at Price. "I'm going to Rawlins and have me a house. I'm going to be a madam. I won't do no work unless I want to."

"Stay in Rawlins until this is settled," Price said. "I may need you to testify when Weston comes up for trial."

"Weston?" Her brows lifted in feigned surprise. "What's he done?"

"I'm sick and tired of you ducking like that," he said sharply. "If you had any feeling for Cronin, you'd want his murderers caught."

She shrugged and walked to a window. "It was a business proposition. We didn't have any feeling for each other. Why should I risk my neck for a man who's dead?"

He was angry then, so angry he wanted to choke the truth out of her. He said, "Looks like I'll have to take you to jail. I'll hold you till you tell me what you know."

"All right, all right," she said sourly. "I don't want to go to your damned jail. That's sure." She stared at the floor. "I suppose you won't believe me, but I don't know anything. I was up late with Cronin the night before. I always sleep till noon on Sundays. I don't know what woke me. Talking, maybe. Or the horses. But when I opened the door, Walt was swinging from that limb and them bastards was riding off. All I seen was their backs. I couldn't identify any of them."

"How'd you get in the willows where we found you?"

"I stood there yelling my head off and scared to death; then the Jarvis kid comes driving around the store like he was going hell for leather. I couldn't think of nothing to do but hide. I figured they'd come back after me, so I ran to the river and hid in the brush. They did come back, and hunted around the store and looked in my cabin. I couldn't hear what they said 'cause I was quite a ways off and the river makes a hell of a racket, but I guess they decided not to hunt for me. They rode up the Yellow Cat, and I didn't see nothing more of anybody till you showed up with De Long."

It could be true. He didn't feel like questioning her any more except to ask, "Who were the four that came back?"

"Weston, Sanders, and the Mohawk brothers, but I didn't see 'em hang Walt. I can't swear to anything in your damned old court. You hear?"

He nodded, and as he turned toward the door she said, "You come see me in Rawlins, Deputy. I'll show you a good time personally."

He went on to his room, saying nothing more to her. Pulling off his gun belt and boots, he sprawled across the bed and fell asleep at once.

Chapter 16

BRUCE JARVIS SAT BESIDE THE CREEK IN A STATE OF INERTIA long after he finished crying. He couldn't blot out of his mind the picture of Walt Cronin hanging from the cottonwood limb. He couldn't silence the nagging voice that kept telling he could have saved Cronin's life if he'd acted soon enough. And he couldn't forget Lizzie's parting words, "Don't you come back here with your tail between your legs looking for help, Bruce Jarvis. You just keep on going."

All this time he'd been planning to run away. Above all things he had wanted to get so far away from the Yellow Cat he would never hear Lizzie's voice again. Now she had sent him away and he didn't want to go.

Oh, he hated Lizzie, all right, but Sam had been kind to him. And Jean? Well, if it hadn't been for her, he just couldn't have stood it the last six years. He didn't want to leave her. He didn't want to leave Susie Farnum, either.

But there was something else, too, something he hated to admit. Fear was a word he didn't want to apply to himself. Fear had kept him from going to Cronin's defense, and he was certain that the shame of that neglect would be with him as long as he lived. Now it was fear again that held him here and kept him from getting on his horse and riding down the creek and on down the river. Out in the open he'd run into the cowmen who had lynched Cronin, or some of their cowboys, and they'd kill him just as certainly as they had killed Walt Cronin.

Finally a restlessness took hold of him. He couldn't remain here and he couldn't go on down the road to the river, so he got on his horse and went upstream. He kept on the west side of the creek except in places where the cliff crowded the water so there wasn't room for the horse. When that happened, he swung off into the Yellow Cat, always returning to the west bank as soon as he could.

He felt safer when there were two screens of brush between him and the road. He didn't want anyone to see him. Lizzie and Sam would think that by this time he was miles away. That was exactly what he wanted them to think.

He was a little above the Potter place when it occurred to him that later in the day the settlers would all be here for Sunday worship and dinner. Maybe Susie would get lonesome for him and wander off toward the creek. If she got far enough from the crowd, he could attract her attention.

He needed to talk to Susie. He wanted to see Jean, too. Maybe she'd be back after a while. While it was dark, he might slip in and talk to Sam. Now he realized the terrible, humiliating truth. He wasn't ready to strike out for himself; he wasn't a man. He needed a family's protection. The Potters weren't his kin, but they were the closest to it of anyone.

He found a brushy side canyon and hid his horse in it, then climbed up the west wall to a ledge that was high enough for him to see over the top of the willows to the Potter yard. He was well hidden, the cliff to his back and a jumble of boulders in front of him.

Hot as it was, he dropped off to sleep. The shots that

killed Lizzie and Sam Potter woke him. He raised his head above the boulders in time to see Cole Weston shoot Red Sanders out of his saddle. Again he was in the grip of a nightmare that couldn't be real, yet it was, so terrifying that he couldn't have moved off that ledge under any circumstances.

He watched the three cattlemen ride away, taking Sanders' body with them. Later he watched the settlers gather, first the Farnums, who found Lizzie's and Sam's bodies, then the Ripleys and the Wagners and the Baileys and the rest. Presently Price Regan came. Bruce saw Regan run into the barn after Susie, and then ride away a short time later.

Several of the men began digging graves. Somebody took a rig and fetched Frank Evans's body. After that there was the burying, the men standing motionless in the evening sunlight with bared heads and the women crying and George Farnum saying a few words.

Bruce couldn't hear anything, but he knew that was the way of it, with Farnum standing a little piece off from the rest. Then they got in their rigs and drove back up the creek, all but Farnum, who stayed. The sun was down and dusk settled upon the narrow valley, and down below Bruce a frog began to croak from somewhere along the edge of the stream.

That was the day, the most terrible day Bruce had ever known. He had only one thing to be thankful for. Jean had not been here when Lizzie and Sam were killed. He didn't know why she hadn't come back or where she was or what had happened to her, but he had a feeling she was alive. He had to believe that. Jean was the only one left. And Susie. Now he had to go, and the only way he could go was up the creek.

Just before the last of the twilight was blotted out by darkness, he worked his way down from the ledge and found his horse. Suddenly he realized he was so hungry he was weak. He remembered the sack of food Jean had fixed and Sam had tied behind the saddle, but when his eager fingers felt for it he discovered it was gone. Sam, in his clumsy haste, had not tied it well.

For a time he stood there, hands clutching the cantle of the saddle, paralyzed by a feeling of absolute helplessness. He wanted to cry again. He could see no future, no hope. Everything had been destroyed today. He couldn't satisfy his hunger. Then the moment of paralysis passed. He had to be on the move.

He tightened the cinch and led his horse down to the creek and let him drink. As far as he was concerned, the country to the north was unfamiliar after he left Wagner's place, but the unknown seemed more promising than the known, for Cole Weston's Rocking C lay that way.

He'd heard Weston talk that morning in the store, he'd seen him shoot Red Sanders, and he knew what everybody said about Weston. No, anywhere was better than downstream where he might run into Weston.

He mounted and, finding a passage through the willows, rode across the creek. He reined up at the Potter barn, wondering if Farnum was still here. There was no reason for him to stay. The chores hadn't taken long and he'd be done before dark. Bruce could find food in the house. The shotgun, too. No reason now why he shouldn't take it. He didn't know what had been done with it, but it was bound to be around somewhere.

He had to concentrate to make any sense out of his thinking. He was in a fog, alive but only half alive. He remained there until his reluctant mind finally worked his problem out. He'd go into the house, silently just in case Farnum was around. He'd run if Farnum was there. He didn't figure out why. It was just that the man didn't have any business there, so his presence represented danger.

He slipped out of the saddle and crossed the yard to the back door. He paused a moment, huddled against the wall. A wild notion started his heart pounding. Lizzie Potter could be killed, but not even a bullet could stop her tongue from wagging. That familiar, strident voice was screaming at him, "Don't you come back here with your tail between your legs looking for help, Bruce Jarvis. You just keep on going."

He had all he could do to keep from running. Then he remembered Walt Cronin saying Lizzie couldn't hurt him except with her tongue. That was true, dead or alive, so he eased forward and opened the screen door. It squealed, agonizingly loud in the night silence. The next instant George Farnum called, "That you, Bruce?"

Bruce's heart started for his throat. He slammed the screen door and whirled and ran. He stumbled over a chunk and fell headlong, scooting on his chin and belly like a sled runner. He heard the screen door slam again and Farnum's heavy tread and his great voice sailing out into the night, "Bruce! I want to talk to you, Bruce. Damn it, where are you?"

He was up again and running. He reached his horse, swung into the saddle and, drumming his heels into the animal's flanks, took off up the road, Farnum's bull voice dying in the distance. He reined up, sucked in a long breath, and then went on again, at a slower pace.

He didn't know why he was so scared of Farnum. He was just scared of everybody now, everybody except Susie. They'd all turn him in, he thought. They were too scared of Cole Weston to hide him. But what about Susie? It would be all right, he decided, if he could see her without Dora knowing about it. He had to trust somebody, and Susie was the only one he could. Hunger was gnawing at him with sharp, animal teeth. She'd get him something to eat. He knew she would.

So, when he reached the Farnum place, he tried again, leaving his horse at the edge of the road and slipping catlike across the yard to the house. Maybe Dora would be up on the rim again with one of the cowboys. Maybe Susie was alone. But how could he find out?

He stopped at the corner of the house, uncertain of his next move. It was black dark now, with no lights in the house. Maybe both girls had gone to bed. If so, he didn't have any chance. He knew the inside of the house almost as well as he did the Potter place. The two girls slept in the same bed in a back room, but he couldn't sneak into the house and try to wake Susie or even tap on a window. He'd get Dora up, too, and then he'd be in a hell of a fix.

He didn't know what first attracted his attention, maybe some faint sound like the swish of a skirt or a toe dragging along the ground, but he suddenly realized that someone was walking toward him from the other side of the house. Susie? Dora? He had no way of knowing which one it was and he couldn't think of any way to find out without exposing himself.

Then Dora solved his problem by calling from a bedroom, "Susie, come in here."

So it was Susie in front of the house. She was coming toward him, then she stopped, and Dora called, "Susie, what are you doing out there?"

"Walking."

"You little fool, if you don't come to bed I'll come out there and get you."

"I'm not keeping you awake," Susie said, angry now. "You're doing it yourself. Go on to sleep."

Dora subsided. Susie came on around the house, and when she was within five feet of him he said in a low voice, "Don't say anything. It's Bruce."

He heard a long breath come out of her, then she leaped toward him, frantic in her relief. Her arms closed around him and she brought his face down to hers and kissed him hard and long. When she let him go, she whispered, "Oh, Bruce, I knew you'd come, I just knew."

"Let's get away from here," he said. "I don't want Dora to know I'm here."

She took his hand and they walked across the yard toward the road where he'd left his horse. When they were far enough away so Dora couldn't hear them, Susie said, "I've got so much to tell you, Bruce. It's been terrible . . ."

"I know," he said. "I was hiding across the creek. I've

been there since morning and now I'm getting out of the country."

"Bruce, you can't go . . ."

"I've got to. They'll kill me if they find me. You know they will. I'm scared, Susie. I'm awful scared."

She squeezed his hand. "We all are. Nobody knows what they'll do next. Maybe they'll murder every one of us."

"Where's Jean? Is she all right?"

"She's in town. She's fine. Regan is taking care of her. Bruce . . ."

"I've got to be riding. I want to be a long ways off by sunup, but I don't have any grub and I don't have a gun. I'm hungry. I haven't had anything to eat all day. I thought maybe you'd . . ."

"I'll get you something." She was standing in front of him, gripping both of his hands in her small ones. "Bruce, there's something I've got to tell you."

"I can't wait. Susie, I tell you I'm hungry. And I need a gun."

"We don't have anything but that old Henry rifle, and Pa would skin me if I gave it to you. I'll slip into the house and find something for you to eat as soon as Dora goes to sleep. You can wait a little longer. Now, Bruce, you listen to me. I talked to Regan today. He's going to arrest Weston, but he needs your help. If you'll testify at Weston's trial and tell what happened when you were in the store this morning, he says Weston will hang."

He couldn't see her face in the darkness. It was just a pale blob, but he felt her hands squeezing his and he heard her rapid breathing. For a long time he couldn't say anything. He simply couldn't believe he'd actually heard her say that, Susie of all people.

Finally the words came out of him, hoarse and incredulous, "You want me to go to town and let everybody know where I am?"

"Yes. It's the only way. Regan says if you run, they're bound to catch you. If they do, they'll kill you. Regan will see you're safe just like Jean. He'll arrest Weston . . ."

"No." It was enough to make him laugh, one man arresting Cole Weston. Susie was crazy, or she just didn't give a damn what happened to him. "That'd be one sure way to get me killed."

"Bruce, you've got to. I'll go with you. I'll ride behind you. None of us will be safe as long as Weston—"

He heard someone coming up the road. Farnum! Panic gripped him. He felt it in his belly. In his knees. He jerked free from Susie's grip and ran to his horse. He heard her desperate cry, "Bruce, Bruce, don't be a fool!"

Then he was in the saddle and drumming the horse's flanks with his heels again and rushing up the creek through the darkness. But the night was not as black as the absolute hopelessness that took hold of him and squeezed him dry of all feeling.

Susie wanted to turn him in. And he had thought she was the one person he could count on. Now there was only Jean.

Chapter 17

PRICE ROSE AT SUNUP MONDAY MORNING, TIRED AND groggy, but very much aware that in a general way the future of Elk River would be decided today, perhaps for as long as a generation. He pulled on his boots and buckled his gun belt around him, and washed in the basin on his bureau, and all the time he was thinking that, in terms of individuals, today was more important than it was to the country as a whole.

Laura and him. The settlers on the Yellow Cat. The Mohawks and Cole Weston. Certainly Barry Madden. If Ralph Carew was here, the old sheriff would tell him that more important than either the country in general or the individuals involved was the broad principle of law.

Would it be an instrument by which justice could be given to all the people in the west end of Tremaine County, or mere words bandied about by Cole Weston, defied by him when it suited his own selfish needs?

That was exactly what Ralph Carew would ask. In many ways he was a tough, uncompromising man, shaped that way by his environment and by the demands which had been made upon him. Yet there was this other side which constantly surprised Price, the way he looked upon law as something over and above the selfish, grasping acts of man. Price was surprised at himself, too, when he realized how much of that idealism had rubbed off on him. That, Carew often said, was the quality which made the difference between a good lawman and one who merely went through the mechanics of his job.

Price put on his Stetson and, picking up his Winchester from the corner of the room, went down the stairs and out of the hotel and lobby into the cool morning sunshine. He could not dispel the gloom that settled upon him. Everything depended upon his finding Bruce Jarvis and bringing him to town, alive and able to talk, and success, he knew, would depend largely on sheer luck.

He ate breakfast in Grandma Spivey's Café. She treated him with cold hostility, saying, "Good morning," when he came in, and nothing else until he finished his flapjacks and had paid her. Then she asked, "Marshal, is that woman going to stay in Saddle Rock?"

"She's leaving on the morning stage," Price said, and left the café.

He saddled his roan, shoved the Winchester into the boot, and took the river road out of town. Every available rider on the Rocking C and Broken Ring would be out on the range searching for Bruce Jarvis today. Weston might, by showing proper sympathy for Red Sanders' death and by blaming it on the settlers, be able to persuade Mrs. Sanders to have her men join in the hunt.

Price still felt reasonably certain that the boy had holed up somewhere along the Yellow Cat. He would be shocked and frightened, and he'd know the search for him would be red hot. But would he remain there today, or would he get panicky and bolt? If he did, Price thought glumly, he'd be dead by noon.

He reached the mouth of the Yellow Cat and turned up

the creek, passing the Evans farm, and stopped at the Potter place. It was deserted. He was angered by this, for he'd told George Farnum to stay, and yet he hadn't actually expected him to obey. By mid-morning, these people would probably be on their way out of the country.

But fifty yards up the road he met Farnum in his wagon. Both stopped, Farnum saying, "Thought I ought to go down and do the chores. How's Jean?"

"She's alive and I aim to keep her that way," Price answered. "Why didn't you stay at the Potter place like I told you?"

"Wasn't no use to," Farnum said defensively. "I'll tell you how it was. I'm thinking the kid must have been purty close yesterday and knew what happened. Anyhow, he stayed hid out till after dark. I reckon he didn't know I was there. He sneaked in, hunting for grub maybe. I was dozing in a rocking chair in the front room when I heard him in the back. I yelled at him, but he took off like a skeered rabbit and that's the last I saw of him."

Price held his tongue, fighting a desire to tell Farnum what a chock-headed idiot he was. If he'd handled it right, he could have got hold of the boy and brought him to town. Or held him till Price arrived, but no, he'd scared him off and now it was hard to tell where he was.

But there was nothing to gain now by cussing Farnum out. He asked, "Which way did the kid go?"

Farnum jerked his thumb up the creek. "He stopped at our place. Leastwise I think he did. Susie won't talk to me. She's mad about something. She's scrapping with Dora fit to kill, but I don't know why. By the time you get there they'll be pulling hair."

"I'll stop and talk to Susie," Price said.

"Regan." Farnum stared down at his big hands that held the lines. "You reckon we oughtta be moving out today? What'll they do to us?"

Again anger flared up in Price. He wanted to say that if a man wasn't willing to fight for his home, he didn't deserve to keep it. But the anger died at once, for he remembered that Farnum had found the bodies of Lizzie and Sam Potter. Against men like Cole Weston and the Mohawks, Farnum had no chance and he knew it.

"I can't tell you what to do," Price said. "I guess it depends on whether I find Bruce alive or not. If I don't, you'll have trouble."

He rode on up the creek, leaving Farnum perplexed and frightened. The last Price saw of him, he was still in the road, afraid even to go on and do the Potter chores.

Before he could dismount in front of the Farnum house, Dora came storming out. "Keep on riding, Regan," she said. "The Jarvis kid ain't here."

He didn't pretend to understand her. All he knew was that he disliked her because of the way she'd jumped him yesterday and beat him on the back. Now he liked her even less. But there was no use arguing with her. He stepped out of the saddle and, leaving the reins dragging, started toward her.

"I ain't gonna let you in the house," she said harshly. "You'll make us nothing but trouble just like the Jarvis boy. He's got Susie so mixed up she don't know what she's doing."

Dora retreated to the doorway and stood there, filling it, a big, coarse-featured girl who was consumed by a fury which seemed to have no cause. When Price continued walking toward her, she screamed, "Get away! Get away! They won't bother us if you let us alone. I don't want to move. Damn it, let us alone. That's all I'm asking."

Susie had been in the bedroom, the door closed, but now, hearing the loud talk, she ran into the room. She called, "I did my best, Mr. Regan. I tried as hard as I could, but he wouldn't go to town."

Price stopped a step from Dora, Susie pausing ten feet behind her. Price said, "I came here to see Susie. Get out of the doorway or I'll give you the back of my hand."

He had never struck a woman in his life, but he would

have then, angered as he was by her senseless behavior. She backed away, her gaze moving from Price to Susie and back to Susie, sullen and resentful at Price's intrusion.

Price nodded at Susie. "Tell me about it."

She struggled a moment for self-control. She had been crying, her cheeks smudged by tears. Her hair had been disheveled, her dress wrinkled, and he had a feeling she hadn't slept all night. It was only then that he realized how disturbed she was, that her whole life revolved around Bruce Jarvis. Half child, half woman, she was in love as much as she would ever be.

When Susie was able to talk, she told Price what had happened, adding, "I just couldn't make him understand, Mr. Regan. When he heard Pa coming up the road, he jumped on his horse and rode away. I don't know where he went, but I don't think he came back this way."

Dora, holding her silence as long as she could, said harshly, "He'd better not come around here. You're better off if you never see him again, you little tart."

Susie whirled on her sister. "You're a good one to be calling me a tart, going up on the rim like you do, with every cowboy you can get and taking fifty cents or a dollar for it. You're worse than Rose ever was."

Dora hit her on the side of the face, knocking her halfway across the room. Price grabbed her before she could strike Susie again and shoved her back against the wall, knowing now why she didn't want him around. She had a business, and she was afraid his presence here would make her lose it.

"I've seen some ornery women in my time, but you win first prize before the judges even take a vote." He jammed her shoulder against the wall with a savage thrust of an open palm. "You're twice Susie's size. If you beat her up, I'll throw you into the jug, and don't you forget it."

"I'll be all right, Mr. Regan," Susie said. "I'll take a

club to her if she hits me again. You go find Bruce. That's all I want."

He waited a moment, his hand still keeping Dora forced against the wall, his eyes meeting hers that were sparkling with the hate she had for him, then he swung around and strode out. Mounting, he rode up the creek, thinking what a no-good, shiftless bunch most of these settlers were.

He stopped at every farm up the creek, but Bruce Jarvis was not to be found. Ripley said he'd heard a horse go by in the middle of the night.

Wagner, who had the last place near the head of the valley, said, "I ain't seen him, Regan, but something happened just before sunup that was gol-dang funny. I heerd the chickens squawking and I figured it was a skunk after one of 'em, so I grabbed my shotgun and ran out the door. I made a lot of noise and reckon he heerd me. Wasn't no skunk. Light was too thin to see for sartin, but I glimpsed something running away from the chicken pen, so I banged away at him. I had a notion it was a bear, but it wasn't. I heerd a horse go lickety-larrup on up the creek. Must have been the kid trying to steal one of my chickens."

Price thanked him and went on, satisfied he was on Bruce's trail. The road petered out at the Wagner farm, and from here on it was barely a path, crossing and recrossing the creek that tumbled down from the plateau to the north in a series of falls.

The climb was a steep one, and Price stopped often to let his roan blow, each time checking the trail for tracks. There was very little travel above the Wagner place, so he felt reasonably certain that Bruce's horse had made the tracks he was following. The boy had been by here not very long before, judging by the sign.

A little over a mile above Wagner's farm Price came out on top, the valley of the Yellow Cat stretching south toward Elk River, a deep twisting cut, the walls widening at the pockets which held the farms, then coming togeth-

er so close that at this distance they gave the appearance
of actually meeting.

The creek ran for miles to the north where it headed
among the high hills that butted up against the sky in a
long rolling line. Bridlebit range lay to the west, and from
where Price sat his saddle he could see the cluster of
buildings. He wondered about Mrs. Sanders and what
she would do, now that she owned a ranch but was a
widow.

The Mohawk spread was to the east. Price could not
see the buildings. He didn't even know their exact
location. From here he could see a few steers carrying the
Broken Ring iron, but no riders were in sight. The
country consisted of a series of ridges and gullies that
were deep enough to hide a man and horse, the ridge tops
covered by cedars that in places grew in tight little
clumps capable of hiding several men.

Price remained there several minutes, letting his roan
rest while he tried to put himself in the boy's place. He
didn't succeed very well, largely because he had no way
of knowing how panicky the kid had become. Price knew
he was hungry. That could enter in, making Bruce keep
going when he might otherwise stop to rest his horse.

If the boy had any reasoning power left, he wouldn't
turn west because the Bridlebit buildings were visible
and he'd know he couldn't go that way without being
seen. He'd probably not turn east because he certainly
must know the Mohawk spread was in that direction,
even if he couldn't see any buildings to remind him of it.
So he might keep right on up the creek which now
rambled noisily along over a stony bottom, the slopes on
both sides rising gently from it.

There was nothing to the north except uninhabited
country for eighty or ninety miles. Once past the head of
the Yellow Cat he'd have difficulty finding water, but the
boy might not know that.

Price considered one other possibility. Bruce might
hide in a clump of willows along the creek or in a cedar

thicket atop one of the ridges, and wait until night to make another run for it. But that seemed unlikely, as hungry as he was. The chances were he'd keep traveling north until his horse dropped. If that was the case, the odds were he'd been caught before this.

For a time Price followed the tracks which kept close to the creek, then he struck a stretch of hard pan and lost them. He swung to the east until he reached the top of the rise, then stopped and, taking out his glasses, searched the country ahead, but caught no trace of anything moving. He knew he hadn't proved anything, for dry washes cut down toward the Yellow Cat, all deep enough to hide several men and horses.

He started north again, gaze moving warily from one side of the stream to the other and now and then touching the ridge tops, a sense of failure weighing heavily upon him.

Then, half an hour later, he came up out of a draw, and topped the next ridge. Directly below him he saw the Mohawk brothers on horses, Bruce standing between them.

Chapter 18

THE MOHAWKS PLAINLY WERE NOT EXPECTING ANY IN-
terference. They had their backs to Price, sitting slack in
leather as if perfectly at ease. The sound of their taunting
laughter came to Price. He heard one of them say
something to the boy, but he was too far away to catch
the words.

Price drew his gun. He would probably have made it
part way down the slope before the Mohawks were aware
of his presence if Bruce hadn't given him away. But the
boy was facing him. Like any kid who had his tail in a
crack one minute and suddenly saw a chance to escape,
he let out a squall. The Mohawk brothers looked around,
saw Price, and whirled their horses and dug for their
guns.

Price cracked spurs to his horse's flanks and went
rocketing down the slope, gun in his hand, shouting,
"Hook the moon! You're under arrest."

But the Mohawk boys had been born to violence; they
were incapable of submitting to arrest even if the shock
of surprise had not set off their hair-trigger tempers.

They both fired, quickly, snap shots that came uncomfortably close, and Price knew at once there was no chance of taking these men alive.

In a startling moment of insight, like the thoughts that whip through the mind of a drowning man, it occurred to Price that it would be a perverse whim of Fate if they killed him and Bruce, and left Cole Weston in the clear without having to turn a hand.

Price didn't cut loose until he had covered half the distance between them. The Bridlebit men fired again, but now their horses were jumpy and both bullets went wide. Price, close now, veered slightly to his left, and let go with his first shot, knocking Joe Mohawk out of his saddle.

Price had purposely held his fire until he was sure he wouldn't miss, but by playing it that way he tipped the scales against him. Tom Mohawk had dismounted. He was an old hand at this, knowing that any shot taken from the top of a horse has to have a broad element of luck to score, especially at a moving target. He was a cold, nerveless man, and now, on the ground, he was bringing his gun up, the hammer back. Price fired and made a clean miss.

If Tom Mohawk had been one second faster, he would have killed Price. As it was, time ran against him. Bruce Jarvis stooped, picked up a rock the size of his fist, and threw it at Mohawk, catching him in the small of the back. It jogged him forward a step and made him miss.

Price pulled his horse up and came out of his saddle in a cloud of dust. For a moment his roan was between him and Mohawk. He stepped into the clear and got in the first shot, the bullet driving through the Broken Ring man's chest. He must have been dead before he hit the ground.

Joe Mohawk, with a bullet wound in his shoulder, had been jarred by the fall from his horse. He hauled himself to his knees by sheer will power. Price heard the boy's cry of warning. Instinct, as much as anything, made him drop flat on the ground, Joe's bullet singing above him.

Because Mohawk was injured his reactions were a little slow. He'd had Price in his sights and he had fired where Price had been, not where he was.

Price let go with a shot, lying flat on his belly. The bullet grazed Mohawk's arm, making a slight flesh wound, but hurting him enough so that his next shot missed. Then Price, with the last bullet in his gun, caught Mohawk squarely in the chest, knocking him off his knees as sharply as if he'd been yanked by a quick, hard tug of a rope.

Price got to his feet and reloaded his gun, staring at the two dead men. Now that it was over, he was weak and aware that sweat was running down his face. He seemed to be fighting for every breath that came to him. He turned and walked away and sat down on a boulder. Cole Weston hadn't won yet.

Price rolled a cigarette, his hands trembling so that he spilled a good deal of tobacco before he got his smoke rolled and sealed and into his mouth. He struck a match, aware that Bruce was standing in front of him, his face deathly pale. He tried to say something, and choked up, no words coming out of his mouth.

"That was close, boy," Price said. "So close I'm not sure whether we're alive or just dreaming we are."

Bruce licked his lips, and this time the words came out. "They was fixing to kill me, Mr. Regan. They was gonna shoot me down just like they done Sam and Lizzie."

"You see that?"

"No, but they said they done it. They bragged 'bout it, like it was something to be proud of. They was playing with me, just having some fun."

That would be the Mohawks, Price thought, playing with the boy the way a cat teases a mouse, squeezing all the pleasure they possibly could out of a killing. Price had never understood how men could be that way, but he'd known several who were, and that included Joe and Tom Mohawk.

Price got up, knowing they had to be on the move.

Some Broken Ring riders might be close enough to hear the shots and come to investigate. He tossed his cigarette to the ground and rubbed it out with his toe.

"They say anything about how Red Sanders got killed?" Price asked.

"No, but I seen it happen. I was across the creek on a ledge, high enough to see over the brush. I guess I was asleep. I heard some shots and poked my head up just when Weston shot Sanders. Lizzie and Sam were both laying on the ground. They was dead."

Price stared at the boy a moment, realizing how much this meant. He laid a hand on Bruce's shoulder. "Now say that over so I'm sure I know how it was. You actually saw Weston shoot Sanders?"

"I said I did. I'd been asleep. I woke up when I heard some shots. They had to be two shots 'cause Lizzie and Sam were dead. I looked just as Weston fired and Sanders fell off his horse."

"What did they do then?"

Bruce scratched his head as if trying to remember. Watching him, Price thought it was a miracle the kid wasn't completely out of his head. Enough had happened to him in the little over twenty-four hours to drive a grown man crazy.

"They loaded Sanders on his horse," Bruce said finally, "and rode off. I didn't see nothing more of 'em, and then pretty soon the Farnums came along and found Lizzie and Sam."

Price turned and, walking to his horse, led him back to where Bruce stood. A strange thing, Cole Weston shooting Red Sanders, and yet maybe it wasn't so strange when he stopped to think about it. He'd sensed from the first that Sanders was the only one of the four with any conscience.

Price was sure he'd never know the whole story, but it was possible that Sanders had been so offended by the Potters' murder that he had said or done something which had provoked Weston into killing him.

"Where's your horse, son?" Price asked.

Bruce lowered his head and stared at the ground. He jerked a hand back toward the creek. "Yonder. On the other side of that brush. I rode him to death." He looked up, his eyes filled with defiance. "I guess you don't know what it is to be scared, but I couldn't think of nothing but to get a long ways from here. I reckon I didn't rest him enough. He just quit and I was on foot when them bastards spotted me. I tried to run, but they got on both sides of me and I couldn't do nothing."

"I've been scared, son," Price said. "You bet I've been scared."

Now shame took hold of Bruce and dragged him down. "But you've never been scared like I was. I'm a coward. I couldn't think of nothing but running."

"You're not a coward," Price said. "There's a hell of a lot of difference between being a coward and being scared. Now take when you heaved that rock. I figure that saved my life, the way things were shaping up."

Bruce swallowed. "I couldn't think of nothing else to do."

"I'll fetch one of the Mohawk horses for you to ride," Price said and, stepping into the saddle, caught one of the horses and led him back to the boy.

He stared at the other horse, fighting his desire to be on the move. Finally he rode to the animal, caught him, and stripped the bridle from him. He gave the horse a belt on the rump with the bridle, knowing he would go back to the ranch, and in time the Broken Ring riders would find the bodies of the Mohawk brothers and take them in.

Jerking his head at Bruce, who was in the saddle, Price led the way back up the slope. Presently Bruce caught up with him. He said, "I'm hungry. I didn't have nothing to eat all day yesterday and nothing today. I went into our house afore I left, but Farnum was there and scared me off. I stopped and talked to Susie, but she couldn't say nothing except that I ought to go to town."

"You'd have been better off if you had," Price said.

The boy turned sullen and was silent, head lowered, one hand grasping the horn. Price prodded, "Wouldn't you?"

Bruce looked up, his pinched face showing his fear. It would be a long time before it left him, Price thought, and he wondered if he could ever get the boy to testify in court.

"I dunno," Bruce mumbled. "I'm in a hell of a fix any way I figure it. I tell you I'm hungry."

"We'll get a meal soon as we hit town," Price promised.

"I ain't going to town," Bruce said. "I'm going back down on the Yellow Cat. I want to see Susie."

"No, you're going to town. I've been thinking about it. I know Susie's worried herself sick about you and I'm sorry we can't let her know you're all right, but there's a chance Weston's got some men along the creek, figuring you'll show up there. You're the key to this whole business, Bruce, and I don't propose for Weston to kill you now."

"I ain't no key," Bruce said, sullen again. "You won't get nothing out of me."

They rode in silence for a long time, Price glancing now and then at the boy's narrow face. He had been starved, neglected and overworked. He wanted to be a man, but he wasn't yet. There was a question when he would be, if an intangible thing like manhood can be dated.

Price's own boyhood had been a difficult one, and he understood how Bruce Jarvis felt, caught between his love for Susie Farnum on one hand, and his hopeless poverty on the other. Add to that the physical danger from which he was not yet free, and it was no wonder he was withdrawn and sullen.

They angled across Broken Ring range toward town, Price alert for other riders, but the ones they saw were distant, momentarily silhouetted against the sky from some ridge top, too far away to be recognized. Presently they reached the last long slant that led down to Elk River, both Weston's headquarters ranch and Saddle Rock visible from the top of the ridge that sloped gently down to the river.

Price pulled up. He said, "We'll get down and stretch."

"I'm hungry," Bruce said doggedly. "You gonna let me starve or . . ."

"I'm hungry too," Price said. "Town's not far off. I figure we'd better rest our horses."

He dismounted. Bruce hesitated, then stepped down, stretching and rubbing his legs. Not used to riding, these last hours had worn him down both physically and emotionally.

Price hunkered on his heels and rolled a smoke. He said, "Tell me what happened in the store yesterday morning."

"I ain't talking to you or in no damned court," Bruce said with dogged stubbornness.

"Why not?"

"'Cause Weston will kill me, that's why. I'm lucky to be alive and I aim to stay alive. Weston's the big shebang around here and I know what'd happen to me if I opened my big mouth."

"All right," Price said. "Just tell me."

So Bruce told him, reluctantly, the story tallying perfectly with what Jean had said. Now, pulling on his cigarette, his eyes on Weston's ranch, Price realized that it would be difficult, perhaps impossible, to convict the rancher of Walt Cronin's killing, but if Bruce would testify, Weston would hang for the murder of Red Sanders.

Everything, then, depended on this boy whose life he had saved. Somehow he had to get through to him and he didn't know how to do it. He thought of talking about his own poverty-stricken background, of how his parents had died and he'd scratched for a bare living, and how he might have headed for hell on high red wheels if it hadn't been for Ralph Carew, who had trusted him and made him a deputy, and in time had given him a set of values by which a man could live.

He thought, too, of telling Bruce about Laura and how much he loved her, and how he was being driven to a break with her father which might make their marriage impossible. He shook his head, sensing that none of these would do.

He rubbed his cigarette out, knowing there was only one thing that might work. He said, "How old are you, Bruce?"

"I'll be seventeen next month."

"Susie?"

"She's just sixteen. She ain't big, so she don't look that old, but she is."

"She's a good girl," Price said. "She loves you."

Bruce lowered his head and was silent. Price said, "I guess you'd like to get married."

"I'm still a kid," Bruce said. "I ain't got nothing. I don't have a home no more."

"I've been thinking," Price said casually. "You'll still live with Jean. The Potter place will go to her. You could marry Susie and take her there."

Bruce looked up. "And have Weston kill us like they done Lizzie and Sam?"

"Weston's going to hang," Price said. "You can see that he does. Then you'll be safe."

You're smart, ain't you?" Bruce flared, "Trying to trick me into talking in your damned old court. Won't work. I'm getting out of the country. I don't know where I'm going, but I'm sure getting out."

"Climb onto your horse," Price said, his patience worn thin. "You said you were a coward and I guess you are. I should think you'd want a chance to show Susie you were a man."

Bruce refused to look at him as he rose and mounted. They rode down the slope and turned toward town. When they reached the first house, they swung off the county road to a side street, Price not wanting the townspeople to know he had found the boy. A moment later they reached the Madden house. Jean, Price thought, was his only chance. If she couldn't make Bruce see what he had to do, no one could.

"Come in," Price said. "Jean's here. She's staying with Laura Madden. I'll have them fix something for you to eat. Then I'm going to put you in jail."

"What for? I ain't done nothing."

"You're a witness," Price said. "I'm going to keep Cole Weston from murdering you if I can. You start running again and he'll get you. The law's the only chance you've got, but you're so damned yellow you won't take it. You can say you won't testify till you're black in the face, but that won't keep Weston from shooting you if he gets a chance."

He laid his words hard against the boy and they hit him with visible force, but he said nothing, following Price up the path to the Madden door, his head down.

Price rang the bell. When there was no answer, he rang again. Still no answer. He began to worry, wondering if Weston's long, murderous arm could have reached this far.

He opened the door and went in, calling, "Laura? Jean?"

But the only sound was the haunting echo of his voice. The house was empty.

Chapter 19

LAURA MADDEN HAD NEVER BEEN CLOSE TO HER FATHER. AS long as she could remember, he had been a self-centered, withdrawn man who had seldom given her more than superficial attention while her mother was alive. His thinking had been fixed on his various projects and enterprises.

The family had drifted through Laura's childhood years from Denver to Central City to Leadville to Cripple Creek to any place where money was being made. Barry Madden, in spite of his ups and downs, always left a place with more money than when he arrived.

Laura's only permanent home, the only house the Maddens had ever owned, was in Saddle Rock. She didn't know why her father had settled here. She had a vague idea it had something to do with Cole Weston, and she knew her mother, who had welcomed this chance to have a home even in an isolated town like Saddle Rock, bitterly opposed the arrangement with Weston.

Over the years Laura's mother had learned to handle

Barry Madden. She catered to his every whim, waiting on him hand and foot, leaning over backward to keep him in a pleasant frame of mind and trying hard to make him feel important. But when it came to things which Mrs. Madden had considered important, such as the social occasions she dearly loved, she went her own sweet way and her husband had to make the most of it.

Now that Mrs. Madden was dead, Laura and her father had been drawn closer together, largely because there were no other relatives within a thousand miles and no close ones at that. Both made concessions, Barry doing the little things for himself that his wife had done for so long, and Laura taking the responsibility of the house. Like her mother, Laura loved parties and she gave a good many, the difference being that now it was the young people Laura's age who came, and before it had been the older ones, the important folks who must be cultivated for the sake of Barry Madden's business and prestige.

Now that Laura thought about it, it occurred to her that Cole Weston and his wife had not been in the Madden house since her mother had died. She remembered that her mother, a charming woman who loved to talk, had trouble being civil to Weston, and Laura remembered, too, how Mrs. Weston would sit apart from the other women in the parlor when the men had gone back to the study.

Mrs. Weston was a quiet, mousy person who kept her eyes on the floor most of the time, never speaking unless she was asked a direct question, and then her answers were usually brief and pointless. She seldom entertained in the big stone ranch house at Rocking C, and when she had, Mrs. Madden went only after much grumbling and groaning, and was always glad to get back when it was over.

Laura had never understood it, but she noticed that when her parents had gone to Rocking C, they hadn't spoken to each other for two days afterward. It proved,

Laura supposed, that Cole Weston had some sort of strange hold upon her father, but she'd never thought much about it until now when she had cause to worry because of Price Regan.

Laura did not attempt to explain her love for Price. She was satisfied to accept and be happy with it, and consider herself lucky to have Price love her. She knew he was not well liked in town and among the cattlemen; she knew he was considered tough and unyielding and implacable. Yet she had never found him that way, for he had a mild, gentle side that few people in this end of Tremaine County realized he possessed.

Of course, there were times when she found him unyielding, too. This situation with Weston and Cronin and Bruce Jarvis was one, and she was certain that Price would die before he would back off from what he considered his duty.

She slept very little Sunday night, worrying about the way things were shaping up. She wondered if she had done right by her father, deciding that she should have tried to follow in her mother's footsteps. Her father loved to dominate, but he never had and he never would dominate Cole Weston. Maybe her mother had done something that had bigger results than Laura had dreamed when she had entertained the important people, particularly the Westons.

Laura was reaching into the darkness for anything that might help Price and her father, but everywhere she looked, it seemed that she could see no one except Cole Weston.

She got breakfast Monday morning with Jean's help and called her father. When he came to the table, he was freshly shaven and dressed as immaculately as ever, but she sensed at once that he was worried to a degree he had never been before in her memory. He was very pale except for the bright red spots on both cheeks. He had the appearance of a man running a high fever.

He refused to touch either the fried eggs or the oatmeal

mush, content with a piece of toast and three cups of coffee. It was all the more unusual because ordinarily he was a hearty eater.

When he rose to go to the bank, she said, "Daddy, I've been thinking about giving a party. Like Mamma used to. Invite people like the Westons."

He looked at her as if she were out of her mind. "At a time like this?" he asked.

"I can't think of a better time."

"Forget it, Laura," he said, and swung on his heels and left the room.

"What's the matter with him?" Jean asked. "Is he sick?"

"I think he is," Laura said. "I think we're all sick."

They were silent a long time, lingering over a final cup of coffee. Laura had known Jean but a few hours. Suddenly it occurred to her that she had never met another girl she liked as well.

She felt perfectly at ease with Jean. They had lived in this house together for less than twenty-four hours, they had slept in the same bed, they had worked together, she had given Jean a dress and stockings and a pair of shoes, and had helped her with her hair. She wondered how she'd ever got along before she'd met Jean. She had been lonely and the days had been long, and the hours with Price had been far too short.

"Jean." Laura put her cup down. "I was just thinking. It's strange that it took a tragedy to bring us together. It's been wonderful to have you here."

"You don't know what it's meant to me," Jean said in a low voice. "Even now I don't know what I'm going to do or where I'll go. Sometimes I thought I hated Ma. She was always nagging and I felt sorry for Pa and Bruce."

She looked down at her cup, fighting back the tears that were constantly threatening since she'd heard of her parents' death. "But now Pa and Ma are both gone and I don't have anything or anybody. Except Bruce, and I'm not sure he's alive."

Laura reached out and put her hands over Jean's. "You've got me, and you're going to stay here as long as you need to."

"It won't be for very long, Laura," Jean said. "You know it won't. Your father doesn't want me here. I guess I can't blame him, toadying around after Cole Weston the way he does."

Laura was indignant for a moment, and angry. She drew her hands back and rose, saying, "Let's get the dishes done." She carried a load of dishes into the kitchen, and it came to her that Jean was perfectly right. Her father ran Saddle Rock, everyone but Price, and yet he did toady around after Cole Weston.

When Jean set the dishes down that she had carried in from the dining room, Laura put an arm around her. "I don't know what's going to happen, Jean, but I have a terrible feeling it's going to be bad, so bad I don't know what I'll do."

"I don't understand," Jean said. "You don't have anything to worry about."

"Would you worry if your father was on one side and the man you were going to marry was on the other?"

"Of course I would," Jean said. "I didn't think of it that way, but I wouldn't have much trouble choosing. Mr. Regan is pretty wonderful, isn't he?"

"Wonderful and stubborn," Laura said, "and maybe born to die before we're married."

"If that happens," Jean said, "it would make anything that has happened to me seem very small and unimportant."

Laura picked up another handful of dishes and carried them into the kitchen. Jean was older and a great deal wiser, Laura thought. Maybe it was because she had so very little in life and therefore appreciated and cherished the tiny bit she did have.

Barry Madden came home late for dinner, but Laura and Jean had waited, keeping the food in the warming oven. He seemed even more distraught than he had been at breakfast, barely picking at his food. When he finally rose, he said, "Laura, come back to the study for a minute."

He left without a word of explanation. It would be about Jean, Laura knew, and when she glanced at Jean she sensed that the other girl knew, too. "I won't be long," Laura said. "You take the dishes into the kitchen."

"Don't fight with him, Laura," Jean said. "Not on my account."

"I think I'll have to fight with him," Laura said, "but it may not be on your account."

Laura went down the long hall to the study and closed the door and leaned against it. She hated the dark and gloomy room, and came here only when she had to clean. Now, watching her father pick up a cigar from the box on his desk and begin to chew on it, she had the weird feeling that the dark tone suited the room, for darkness belonged to the devil, and she was convinced that her father had sold himself to the devil as surely as Cole Weston was the devil.

"I'm sorry about what I'm going to have to say, Laura," Madden said, striding back and forth and chewing nervously on his cold cigar. "I've been afraid it would come to this, but I didn't want to hurt you. If I had my way, I would give you anything in the world I could, but sometimes circumstances force us to take steps we don't want to take."

He paused and, removing the cigar from his mouth, looked at it, and then replaced it, moving in a jerky fashion as if Cole Weston were tugging at the strings that controlled him.

"I talked to Price about this yesterday and he defied me, so I have no choice. He left town early this morning. I haven't seen him today, so I don't know where he went or what he's doing, but I presume he's hunting for that Jarvis boy. If he finds him and brings him to town, then we've got more trouble than we could dream of."

He tongued his cigar to the other side of his mouth. "Pete Nance is in town waiting for Price. I understand this is personal, due to some difficulty they had at the Rocking C, and was postponed because Cole didn't want any fighting out there. It would have disturbed his wife. Curly Blue is in town, and if Price shows up with the Jarvis boy Blue's supposed to notify Cole, who will come in with some of his men. Apparently they have reason to think that the Jarvis boy shot and killed Red Sanders. It's all tied in with this rustling that's been going on for months and which Price refused to stop."

Laura watched him, a sick foreboding taking hold of her. She knew what was coming. She wouldn't have to choose freely between her father and Price. Her father was forcing a single choice upon her.

"Now this is the part I hate to say," Madden went on. "We had a meeting of the town council today and took the town marshal's job away from Price and gave it to Max Harker. As soon as possible, I'm going to contact Ralph Carew and have him recall Price, if he's still alive, which is doubtful if he fights Pete Nance. I told Price he wasn't going to marry you, so don't see him. And you'll have to get rid of the Potter girl. I don't care what the excuse is. Just get rid of her."

Laura stared at her father with utmost loathing. He seemed a stranger to her, a man she had never really known, a man without conscience and a coward who had surrendered everything to Cole Weston.

"What have you done that Weston knows about?" she asked. "He must have some hold on you."

"Nothing," he said. "Don't talk to me that way. I'm doing what I have to do."

"No, you're not," she said sharply. "He killed Jean's mother in cold blood. Her father, too. And Walt Cronin. Maybe Bruce Jarvis. Maybe even Price by now. What's happened to you that you can stand here and take his side and—and defend him in everything he's done?"

"I'm not going to argue with you," he said in cold fury. "Just do what I tell you."

"I'm eighteen and I won't do anything you tell me

except leave this house," she said in a detached voice that did not sound like her own. "If you think I'll give Price up for a minute, you're crazy. I suppose you're my father, but father or not, you're not worth a single short hair on the back of Price Regan's neck."

She whirled and opened the door and ran out, slamming it behind her. She went on into the kitchen, calling, "Jean, help me pack. We're leaving."

"Laura, I said not to—"

"Not on your account," Laura said. "Price's."

She went upstairs to her room, Jean following reluctantly. Laura laid two suitcases on the bed and began throwing clothes into them, careless in her hurry. Suddenly she said, "I'll go live with you, Jean. At least we'll have a roof over our heads. I'll work. Maybe Bruce will come back. If he doesn't, we'll run the farm."

Crazy talk born of desperation, but Jean didn't tell her that. They filled both suitcases and sat on them to latch them. Laura fumbled in a bureau drawer for her handbag. She didn't have much money. A little of her own. A few dollars her father had given her a day or two ago to buy a dress with. The house money, or what was left of it. She put it all together in one purse, a little better than thirty dollars.

"That's all we've got," Laura said.

Then she remembered the jewel box and crammed everything that was in it into her purse. Her mother's diamond ring and gold watch would be worth quite a bit if she had to sell them. She whirled, nodding at Jean, and went down the stairs.

Her father was waiting in the hall. "Don't do this," he said.

"I can't help it," Laura flung at him. "What choice have you given me?"

He was red in the face and embarrassed, but he made himself say, "You've got one choice. Don't go out to the Yellow Cat."

She knew what he meant. "One murder leads to

another, doesn't it? I guess you'd know better than anyone else except Weston."

She left the house without waiting for any more argument from him. Once outside in the harsh afternoon sunlight, Jean said, "We can't go out there, Laura. We'd be killed just the way Ma was. Let's wait till Mr. Regan gets back."

"I guess we'd better," Laura said. "We'll get a room in the hotel."

A sense of caution prompted Laura to take the alley and go into the hotel from the back. She had Jean climb the stairs that led up from the alley door, then she went down the hall to the lobby and signed the register, ignoring the clerk's questioning look. She took the key and hurried up the stairs, motioning for Jean, who was waiting in the hall, to follow her. Her room overlooked the street. As soon as she locked the door, she ran to the window.

Jean came to her and put her arm around her waist. "Laura," she said, "I'm sorry."

"I'm sorry too," Laura said bitterly. "If Price is killed today, I'm worse off than you are. I'll never go back home."

They stood there for a time, both girls utterly miserable, their eyes on the street. Barry Madden appeared and went into the bank, walking in that strange jerky fashion which was natural with him when his nerves were taut. Curly Blue left Max Harker's store and cruised along the sun-warped plank walk with his bow-legged gait.

Presently Pete Nance appeared in the door of Mahoney's Bar, holding back the bat wings as he looked out upon the street. A killer, Laura thought, who had taken upon himself the authority of God, the right to take life with the guns he carried in the tied-down holsters on his hips. He seemed amused and a little superior to everyone and everything in this little town where his work had called him. He stepped back and let the swing doors flap shut.

"I wish we had a gun," Laura said. Then she knew she just couldn't stay here and let Price ride in to be killed. "I'm going out. No matter what happens, stay here. Keep the door locked."

She unlocked the door, waited until she heard the key turn, then hurried down the stairs and out of the lobby. Curly Blue was standing in front of the drugstore smoking a cigarette, his appreciative eyes on her. She hurried across the dusty street and went into Harker's store. He was rearranging some bolts of cloth on the dry-goods side of the store, and when he turned she saw he was wearing a star and carrying a gun under his waistband.

"I want to talk to you, Max," she said.

He bowed, smiling. "I can't think of any lovelier person that I could talk to." He saw that she was staring at the star on his shirt. "I'm sorry to have to take Price's job. I didn't want it and I can't do it justice."

"That's what I want to talk to you about," she said. "You've got to help Price. Pete Nance is in town."

"I know," Harker said.

"So is Curly Blue, and he's to bring Weston and his crew into town when Price shows up. He can't fight them all, Max. You've got to help."

The cynical smile that was so typical of Harker appeared on his lips. "A man has an inalienable right to choose death if he so chooses. Price has. I warned him, but he wouldn't listen. I've been dying for years, Laura. Maybe it'll catch up with me tomorrow, but wouldn't I be foolish to go out of my way to hasten it?"

"You won't help him?"

He shrugged. "You haven't given me any reason why I should."

She whirled away from him. Harker said, "Laura."

She turned back. "I envy Price," Harker said. "I wish someone, just anyone, loved me the way you love him."

She walked out of the store, not looking back at Harker, whose eyes followed her until she was in the street. Now it occurred to her that Price might stop at her house, and she wanted him to know where she was. She'd leave a note on the slim chance he would find it before anyone else did.

Walking so fast she was almost running, she crossed the vacant weed-covered lot between the hotel and the drugstore. A moment later she could see her house. Two horses were in front. One was Price's roan. She cried out involuntarily and then she did run toward the house as fast as she could.

Chapter 20

PRICE WALKED THROUGH THE MADDEN HOUSE, WORRIED AND puzzled by Laura's and Jean's absence. He had told Jean plainly she must stay here and she had promised she would. Laura, he was sure, would have made her stay, even if Jean had been inclined to leave. To make it worse, he had intended to leave Bruce Jarvis here, too, thinking that Barry Madden's house was the safest place in town for the boy.

He paused in the dining room, staring perplexedly at the table which hadn't been completely cleared of dirty dishes. Bruce darted around him and, grabbing a slice of ham, wolfed it down. Then Price heard someone come in, and Laura's cry, "Price, when did you get here?"

He whirled toward her as she ran into the room, and for a moment they had no time or thought for anyone but each other. When Laura released him and tipped her head back to look at him, he saw the tears that were in her eyes, and he realized how much pressure worry had put upon her these last hours.

"I just got here," he said. "I was sure wondering where you and Jean had gone."

She didn't hear him. She just stood there looking at him as if her eyes could not get enough of the sight of him, then she whispered, "I've been afraid, Price. Terribly afraid."

"Everything's fine," he said. "I've got the boy." He motioned toward Bruce who stood at the table shoving bread and ham into his mouth as fast as he could; then he picked up a glass of milk and drank it without taking it from his lips. "Bruce, this is Laura Madden. Jean's been staying with her."

Glancing around, Bruce bobbed his head as Laura said, "I'm pleased to meet you, Bruce." He wiped a sleeve across his mouth and reached for another piece of ham.

"He hasn't had anything to eat for two days," Price said.

"Oh, I'm sorry," Laura said. "I'll find you something, Bruce. There isn't much on the table."

She took the pitcher and ran through the kitchen into the pantry, filled it with milk from a crock, and returned to the dining room with it and a wide slab of dried apple pie. Bruce grabbed the pie and ate it from his hands, some of the filling squeezing out onto his fingers. He wiped his hands on his pants, then filled the glass with milk and drank it, his hands trembling with weariness.

"It's been rough," Price said. "He was ducking around all day yesterday trying to keep out of everybody's way and this morning he ran into the Mohawk boys. I got there in time to save his hide, but it was a close shave."

Laura stood beside Price, her arm on his as she stared at the boy. He seemed all eyes and stomach. With his pinched face and shaggy hair and wornout clothes that were too big for him, he seemed even more than Jean to have suffered from the miseries of poverty.

Suddenly Laura remembered why she was here, and she gripped Price's arm. "We can't stay. I got so excited when I saw your horse outside that I forgot. I quarreled with Daddy. Jean and I have moved out to the hotel."

That was crazy, Price thought, and yet, as he looked down at Laura's pale face, he found he was not as surprised as he had thought he would be when he first heard what she said. He asked, "Over me?"

"Partly," Laura said. "And over Jean. He told me to get her out of the house. But it's more than that, Price. It's something bigger. I've heard about people selling their souls. Is that just preacher talk, or could a man really do that?"

"I don't know," Price said thoughtfully, remembering how Barry Madden had been his usual poised, domineering self on Saturday morning in the bank, but yesterday, here in the hall of his own house, he had been a harried, uncertain man, giving orders he must have known would not be obeyed.

"They've fired you from the deputy's job," Laura said, "and Harker has the star. Pete Nance is in town. So is Curly Blue, and he's supposed to ride out to the Rocking C as soon as you get here. I guess Weston wants to know if you found Bruce."

Price grinned. "Well, let's tell him."

"But you can't fight Pete Nance," Laura cried. "Can't you see that? You know why Weston brought him here?"

"Well, I can't disappoint him."

"Let's go to the hotel," Laura said. "Jean's there alone. I'm worried about her. She'll want to know about Bruce, too."

Price nodded and took Bruce by the arm. "We're going to see Jean," he said. "I'd better get you out of here before you founder yourself. You're worse'n a cow in an alfalfa patch."

Bruce belched and rubbed a sleeve across his mouth again, looking a little sick. He went along without resisting, Price wondering about the horses and deciding to leave them where they were for the moment. It was just as well that no one knew Bruce was here until Price was ready to show his hand.

He still had not thought of a way to make the boy talk,

but that wasn't anything to worry about now. The immediate problem was to get Cole Weston locked up in jail. Price, first of all a realist, had no illusions about the difficulty of the job that faced him.

"We'll walk," Price said, keeping a hand on the boy's arm.

Bruce glanced at Price, his mouth tightening. His old fears were plaguing him again, his eyes as wary as those of a hunted animal, but still he didn't hang back or fight Price's grip on his arm.

The three of them went into the hotel through the back door and up the stairs, no one seeing them, as far as Price knew. There was never much activity on the tag end of a hot Monday afternoon in Saddle Rock, but today there seemed less than usual. The word had got out, Price thought, and people were staying off the street.

Laura tapped on the door, calling, "It's Laura, Jean." The girl opened the door at once. Price shoved Bruce into the room ahead of him. For a moment Jean stared at the boy as if she couldn't believe he was actually here, then she cried out, and took him into her arms and hugged him.

"Bruce, Bruce," she whispered. "What happened? Where have you been?"

"It's quite a story," Price said, stepping into the room behind Laura and shutting the door.

He crossed to the window and looked down into the street. No one was in sight except Curly Blue, who lounged indolently in the shade of a wooden awning. Presently Pete Nance appeared in the doorway of Mahoney's Bar and looked up and down the street in the disdainful way he had, and stepped back.

When Price turned, he saw that Jean had pulled Bruce down on the side of the bed and was sitting with an arm around him, tears running down her face but making no sound with her crying. She wiped her eyes and said in a low tone, "We're all that's left, Bruce."

If anyone could make the boy talk, it would be Jean.

Price said, "He saw Cole Weston shoot Red Sanders yesterday, but he's too big a coward to stand up in court and swear to what he saw. It's up to him whether Weston hangs."

"He's not a coward," Jean said angrily. "You aren't, are you, Bruce?"

The sullen expression that Price had seen so often on the boy's face was there now. He said, "I ain't a coward, but I ain't no damn' fool, neither. Maybe I was a coward when they dragged Walt out o' the store, but I can't do no good now by blabbing what I seen."

"What about Ma and Pa?" Jean asked. "Where were you . . ."

"Hiding across the creek," Bruce answered. "I reckon I was asleep. I heard some shots, and when I looked Lizzie and Sam were dead."

"Tell the rest of it," Price said.

The boy threw him an angry glance, then said sullenly, "Weston shot Sanders. I seen it, but that don't mean I'm going to the county seat and wait around till they try Weston and then get up in court and tell what I seen."

"What do you think you'll be doing between now and then?" Price demanded.

"I dunno," Bruce said. "I'm going somewhere."

"Maybe you'd better go ask Weston for a job so you'll be handy," Price said. "You know he'll kill you if he's not in jail."

"Not if he don't catch me he won't," Bruce said stubbornly.

"What will Susie say?" Jean demanded. "Bruce, you just aren't thinking straight. We've got to go home. It's the only place we can go. We'll make out, you and me. Susie, too, if you want to fetch her there."

Bruce didn't say anything. He sat on the bed, hunched forward, his big-knuckled hands clenched on his lap. Jean looked up at Price and shook her head. "He'll see what he's got to do, Mr. Regan. You'll have to give him some time."

"I hope he sees it," Price said. "I saved his life today. He owes me something, and he owes a lot more to Walt Cronin and your folks. He owes plenty to you and your neighbors on the Yellow Cat and that girl Susie. Looks to me like he's not worth her little finger, but she's sure in love with him."

Price gave them his back and looked out of the window again. Barry Madden had just left the bank and was going into the jail. Curly Blue was still under the wooden awning. Might as well get it over with, Price thought.

There was only so much waiting a man could stand, and Price had a feeling that Nance could endure the waiting better than he could. The gunman was the biggest obstacle that stood between Price and Weston. Later there would be Weston and some of his Rocking C hands, Curly Blue in particular, but he wouldn't worry about that now.

He turned to Laura. "Will you go tell Curly I'm here and I've got Bruce?"

She met his eyes, hesitating, then asked, "Are you sure that's the right thing to do?"

"I'm sure," he said.

"All right, I'll tell him."

"Good." He smiled as if there were no great importance attached to what he was asking her to do. "I'll take the horses to the stable. Jean, I want you to keep Bruce here. I don't know what Weston will do when he hits town, but he's got to the end of his string. With the murders he's got behind him now, one or two more won't make any difference."

Bruce, aware he was making a bad showing to all of them, burst out, "What good will it do anybody if I do what you're ding-donging me to do? We can't last without Walt and his store. Chances are folks are moving off the creek now."

"Maybe," Price said, "but what your neighbors do has got nothing to do with what you and Jean do. And there's something else I reckon is the most important of all.

Something you haven't learned but I have. I was older than you when I learned it. Maybe I never would have learned it if I hadn't been taught it by a good man named Ralph Carew. I'd like to do for you what he done for me, but maybe you just don't have enough sand in your craw."

Price walked to the door and opened it, motioning for Laura to leave. She stepped into the hall, and Price was over the threshold before Bruce asked in a ragged voice, "What was it?"

"Lock the door, Jean," Price said. He gave the boy a searching look, not at all sure there was anything in the kid to tie to. After all, that was the real answer, the intangible qualities inside a man that make him do the things he does. Sometimes you couldn't put your finger on them. Why was Weston driven to follow the path he had chosen? Or Barry Madden, even to the place where he had lost his daughter?

"Funny thing, the way it's worked out," Price said. "You've got the future of this town and Elk River Valley in your hands, Bruce. This whole section of Colorado, as far as that goes. And a lot of other people who need homes and will find them here someday."

"What was it you learned?" Bruce cried.

"I learned that a man who can't look at himself in the mirror and be a little proud of what he sees there just ain't no man at all. Right now you can't, so you'll run and you'll keep on running. Someday maybe you'll wind up shooting yourself, and nobody, Jean or Susie or nobody, will give a good thin damn."

Price went out and shut the door. Laura put her hands up to his cheeks in a gentle caress. "Do you have to look into the mirror?"

He nodded. "But there's something more important to me than that. I've got to live so you can look at me."

She kissed him and she let him see how proud she was of him, then she whirled, her skirt flowing away from her ankles, and went down the front stairs. Price left through

the back, walking to the Madden house, and, mounting
his horse, led the other animal to the rear of the livery
stable. He called, "Barney?"

De Long came out of the tack room, hurrying along
the runway. "Price, where the hell you been?"

"Fetching in Bruce Jarvis," Price said. "Take care of
these horses, will you?" When De Long reached for the
reins, Price added, "I hear Pete Nance is in town."

"He's gunning for you," De Long said. "This is a hell
of a bad deal, boy. If you get him, you've still got to buck
Weston, and he's got a pretty salty bunch. Curly Blue, for
one. He ain't gonna forget the licking you gave him. The
odds are too long, Price. You can't win."

"I've got to try," Price said. "Looks to me like I'll be
trying alone."

De Long retreated a step. "I'll take care of the horses."

Price made a careful check of his gun. He wasn't at all
sure he could take Nance, but he had put in hours of
practice because Ralph had demanded it. If he won, he
felt there was a chance that Cole Weston and his bunch
would cave. A slim chance, but still a chance, for Pete
Nance represented a big investment on Weston's part, an
investment aimed to take care of exactly this kind of
situation. So it was better to jump Nance now and not
wait.

But when he stepped into the street, Max Harker
called from the jail doorway, "Price, come here."

Price hesitated, for he was geared to face Nance now,
and this interruption meant that the meeting must be
postponed. Then Harker said, "Come here. Barry wants
to see you."

So Price turned toward the jail, even then not sure he
was right. He stepped into the jail office. Harker shut the
door behind him. Madden sat at the desk that had been
Price's from the time he had come to Saddle Rock.
Madden got up slowly. He was a sick man, maybe a crazy
man. He walked around the end of the desk, his hands
trembling.

Price glanced at Harker, who was wearing a star and had a gun under his waistband. Price sensed that this was trouble and not the kind he wanted. No matter how it turned out, it would not answer the problem that faced him, and he wasn't sure what Harker would do. Now the man turned to the gun rack and took down a shotgun.

"Price," Madden said, "you're a fool. The worst kind of a stupid fool. I told you to let this alone but you wouldn't listen."

He stood ten feet from Price, his hands trembling more violently than ever, then, without warning, he lunged at Price, swinging a wild blow at Price's head.

Chapter 21

PRICE HAD NOT HEARD OF BARRY MADDEN FIGHTING WITH anyone. Knowing Madden as well as he did, this attack was the last thing he expected. Surprise held him inactive for a moment so that he barely ducked the blow in time.

Price said sharply, "Stop it, Barry!" and backed up a step; then it flashed through his mind that Max Harker had shut the door and picked up a shotgun. Maybe this was a trap and they aimed to kill him.

But Madden didn't stop. He cursed Price in a steady monotone and tried to hit him again. Harker, standing by the gun rack, didn't say or do anything. Price, his patience frayed and seeing no excuse for this, blocked Madden's inept blow, and cracked him on the jaw with a hard right that stretched the banker flat on his back on the jail floor.

"That was a good punch, Price," Harker said. "Funny how a man goes out of his way to get a wallop like that."

Madden raised himself on an elbow and stared at Price as if puzzled by what had happened. Price backed up to the wall so he could watch both Madden and Harker. Madden could be carrying a gun, and as crazy as he was, he might try to use it. But the wildness in him seemed to have passed. He just lay on the floor, blinking and rubbing his jaw.

"What are you doing with that shotgun, Max?" Price asked.

"I'm the town marshal," Harker said. "Seems to me that one of my duties is to keep the town from being shot to hell. That could happen. Curly Blue just left town. He'll have Weston here along with as much of the Rocking C crew as Weston can get hold of in a few minutes."

Price gave Harker a close look, not quite sure what was in the storekeeper's mind. Maybe he was promising help, or maybe he was giving a warning not to start any shooting.

"I don't get it, Max," Price said. "You're a counter jumper. You're 'way over your head, with things stacking up the way they are."

"I'm the best there is." Harker nodded at Madden, who was still on the floor. "I'm a better man than he is." He went to the desk, filled his pockets with shells, broke the shotgun and saw that it was loaded, then snapped it shut and moved to the door. "I'm going outside and let you have a talk with Barry."

Harker opened the door and paused, looking back at Price, the familiar, cynical smile on his lips. "I guess we just want to play big. That's Barry's trouble. And Weston's. Well, the star makes me big, doesn't it?"

He went out, closing the door. Price said, "Get up, Barry. Sit there at the desk. Looks like it's past time for us to have a talk."

Madden got up, still rubbing the bruise on his jaw, and sat down at the desk. That one blow had made a changed man out of him. The arrogance, the smooth, confident manner, the desire to dominate: the characteristics that Price had disliked in him so much now seemed to be gone. Instead, there was a kind of wonder as if he couldn't believe this had happened to him.

"Nobody ever hit me before," Madden said.

"Maybe you never took a swing at another man before," Price said. "Did you expect me to stand there and let you beat hell out of me?"

"I don't know," Madden said. "I guess I never thought about it."

Price knew he had to hunt Pete Nance down and brace him; he had to drive the man out of town or kill him. But set against that knowledge was the feeling that for the first time since he had met Barry Madden, the man had been humbled enough to talk. He had never understood why Madden had followed the ruthless course Weston had led. Suddenly Price made his decision. It was important that he find out what prompted Barry Madden. Nance could wait.

"Laura's left you," Price said, "and not just because of me. She's all you've got, but you drove her out of your home. She's fair. She knows what you've done and what Weston's done, and she likes Jean. Why did you do it?"

With the door closed, the interior of the jail was stifling. Madden got out a white handkerchief and wiped his face. He remained silent.

"Walt Cronin was lynched," Price said. "Maybe he was guilty. I think he was, but just the same he had a right to a fair trial, as fair a trial as Weston is going to get. I think you knew all the time what Weston aimed to do, but you've gone right on supporting him. Why?"

Madden wiped his face again. Still he said nothing.

"Bruce Jarvis was a witness to that lynching," Price went on. "Weston and the rest rode up the Yellow Cat. One of them murdered Frank Evans. They went on up the creek and killed Sam and Lizzie Potter in cold blood. I'm not sure who did it, but I do know that Weston murdered Red Sanders. I have an eyewitness to it. I don't know why Red was killed, but I can guess. I think he balked at the Potter killing. Maybe Weston figured they had to get rid of him for their own protection. That's the way murder is, Barry. The first one very often sets off a series of killings."

Price paused. Madden stared at the desk top. He wet dry lips with the tip of his tongue and wiped his glistening face with his wadded-up handkerchief, but remained silent.

"I think you know Jean Potter would have been killed if they'd found her at home," Price went on. "They'd still kill her if they could find her. They'll tear your house apart to get her if they think she's there. Maybe Laura will get killed, too. That's the kind of man Cole Weston is, Barry, and you've known it all the time."

If Price lived, this man would be his father-in-law. Anger swelled in him until it became fury, and he laid his tongue on the man as if it were a quirt. "What are you, Barry? Do you think Laura has any right to be proud of you? Weston's sent the word out to kill the Jarvis boy so he can't talk, but he failed. I've got him, Barry. I killed both the Mohawk boys because I had to keep Bruce Jarvis alive as a witness. Think of it. Cronin. Frank Evans. The Potters. Red Sanders. The Mohawks. Seven people killed since Sunday morning, and Cole Weston is responsible for every one of them. That makes you responsible, too. Why, Barry? God damn it, talk!"

Madden started to get up and fell back. White-faced, he said, "All right, Price. I'll tell you. It's like Max Harker said a while ago. I had to be big."

Madden took a cigar out of his pocket and began to chew on it. "The only thing that really hurts is that I've lost Laura. I'll get her back if I have to crawl to do it. Even if she marries you, I'll get her back."

He leaned forward, fists clenched, his eyes on Price. "I've always had a talent for making money. I got started selling gadgets on Denver street corners, making my pitch to any crowd I could get. I did pretty well. Then I headed for the mining camps. I took my wife with me. I gambled some. As soon as I had enough money, I began dealing with mining stock. After Laura was born, I kept on, doing a little better all the time.

"We kept moving. Central City. Leadville. Aspen. The

San Juan camps. Cripple Creek. I lost sometimes but I always came back. If I'd stayed there, I'd have been a rich man by now, but it wasn't what I wanted."

Madden took the cigar out of his mouth and laid it on the desk, then he tipped his head and stared at the cigar, a minute ticking by before he went on, "This is something you can't understand because you don't want the things I want."

Madden paused, frowning, then he added, "No, that's wrong. You just naturally get what I want. You don't have to seem to be something you aren't. You don't have to scratch like hell to get it. Call it power. Or prestige. Or respect from everybody who knows you. That's what I had to have and I couldn't get it living the way I was. Money didn't buy it for me."

Madden lifted his head and stared at Price with resentment. "You're too God-damned honest. Or maybe you've got a sense of duty. I don't know what it is, but it's something that made Laura love you. It makes Harker stand up for you. It's even made Weston afraid of you. That's why he's been ding-donging me to get rid of you."

He swallowed, the bitterness growing in him. "But me, I never had it, not till I came here. I met Weston in Denver and he told me about this country and how it needed a bank, and how we'd have things the way we wanted them if we worked together. We'd get a new county made and I'd go to the legislature. Maybe I'd go to Congress in time. Why, I might even get to be governor."

Madden began to tremble again. He stood up and put his hands palm down against the desk. "He gave me a dream, a dream you'll never understand. Politics was the answer to what I wanted, and with Weston behind me I'd have it. He was ready to move at the next session of the legislature. We'd get our county and I'd be on my way. But you've spoiled it, Regan. You've spoiled it all and you've taken Laura away from me."

He sat down and wiped his face, but still it glistened with beads of moisture. Price, staring at him, understood far better than Barry Madden thought he did, and so he had only contempt for him.

"You've called me a fool a good many times, Barry," Price said, "but you're a bigger fool than I could ever be. You've thrown in with a murderer and you'll never be free from it as long as you live. I say you're a fool because if you'd quit Weston and helped open Elk River Valley to settlement you'd have had enough people here to have made this a county, and you'd be in the legislature by now."

Price stopped. What was the use of talking? The only good thing he could say about Barry Madden was that he was Laura's father. He shivered, even in the heat of the jail office. He could feel the bitter wind that had begun to blow years ago when Cole Weston and Barry Madden had first formed their partnership in Denver. Now it was a gale of hatred and resentment and greed, and even after Madden had told him this, as honest as he could possibly have been, he apparently felt no guilt, no shame. Just the bitterness of a man who had lost a dream and hated the one who had taken it from him.

Turning, Price opened the door and stepped out into the late afternoon sunshine. Max Harker stood at the corner of the jail building, the shotgun in his hand. He said, "They're coming, Price. Five of them."

Price had waited too long. Pete Nance was in the saloon, very much alive, the insurance Cole Weston had taken out for this very emergency. Then the thought was in Price's mind that if he died today, Barry Madden could still have his dream. But what of Laura who had left her father? And Jean and Bruce Jarvis and all the settlers on the Yellow Cat and the people who might someday find homes here? What of Ralph Carew who had sent Price to Saddle Rock to do a job, who believed that law was the instrument by which all men could be given justice?

Price watched them ride into town, Cole Weston in front, Curly Blue behind him, the other three strung out along the dusty street. Five of them, all right. Too many, with Pete Nance over there in Mahoney's Bar, an unrepentant Barry Madden behind him, and the only possible help that which might come from a storekeeper who was a sick man. Even that help was not assured. When he looked at Harker's pale face, the two bright red spots on his cheeks, he was even less sure of his help.

Weston and his men dismounted at the first hitch rack they came to. Price knew they had seen him, and again he felt the bitter wind blowing down this strip of dust that Saddle Rock called a street, the bitter wind of death and defeat and a lost future. For a moment Price thought of Laura and of his life with her, and suddenly temptation was strong to turn and walk away from this. He could. It wasn't too late.

But it lasted only a moment. Strangely enough, it was Barry Madden's words that brought into sharp focus what Price Regan must do. "You're too God-damned honest. Or maybe you've got a sense of duty. I don't know what it is, but *it's something that made Laura love you.*"

Honesty or duty or whatever Ralph Carew would call it, but the point was that without it he would never have had Laura's love; without it he would never keep her love.

He stepped into the street and faced them. They made a line from one edge of the boardwalk to the other. Five of them, moving toward him! Too many, even without Pete Nance over there in Mahoney's Bar. Too many, but this was the hand he had been dealt. Now he had to play it out.

"You're under arrest, Weston," Price said. "For murder. If any of your men make trouble, you'll be the first one to die."

The Rocking C men stopped, Curly Blue grinning defiantly. From the front of Mahoney's Bar Pete Nance called, "You're making a mistake, Regan, a hell of a bad mistake. I'm going to kill you."

Chapter 22

So this was the way it had been planned. Cole Weston had known all the time that with his Rocking C crew and Barry Madden's help, he could handle the people who lived here, but he had also known Ralph Carew, known him well enough to be sure that he couldn't handle the deputy Carew had sent here to tame Elk River Valley. Pete Nance had been hired for one purpose: to kill that deputy.

For a moment Price regretted that he had wasted time in the jail listening to Barry Madden, time he could have used to have taken care of Pete Nance. Now he had to draw on the gunman, had to kill him or be killed, and while he was doing that, Weston or Curly Blue or some of the others could shoot him in the back.

But he had no choice. Harker might keep Weston and his men out of it. Price didn't know, but he did know that the instant he started to turn or made a motion of any kind, Nance would go for his gun.

So Price made his decision. He drew as he swung around to face Nance, the lightning-fast, smooth draw that Ralph Carew had taught him, and Carew had been a hard man to satisfy. For one horrible moment Price thought he had been too slow. Nance had his gun almost free of leather when Price turned, a time advantage that let him get off the first shot.

Price saw the flash of Nance's gun, a sharp tongue of flame leaping into the shadow thrown across the street by the false front of the saloon; he heard the sound of the shot and the slap of the slug into the wall behind him, and the echoes of that shot were thrown back from one false front to the other.

But Nance was too fast to be accurate, and so he died, with Price's shot hammering into the echoes of Nance's. The gunman was knocked off his feet by the bullet. Price shot him again as he fell and whirled to face Weston and his men. He didn't need to worry about Nance. The man was dead.

Cole Weston and his cowhands remained motionless. Harker had them under his shotgun, but he couldn't cover all of them. It was surprise that held them motionless rather than the fear of Harker's shotgun. Price saw it in Weston's face, the stark naked surprise of a man who had just seen something so unbelievable and terrifying that he was paralyzed by it.

"Drop your gun belts," Price said. From the edge of his vision he saw men moving out of the saloon toward Nance's body. He called, "Let him lie there. I want Weston to get a good look at him."

He kept his gaze pinned on Weston's face. He'd kill the cowman if he made a move toward his gun, and Weston must have sensed it. He remained absolutely motionless. Price said, "I won't give you all day. If you submit peaceably, you'll go to the county seat and get a fair trial and a legal hanging. If you resist, I'll kill you. It doesn't make any difference to me because you'll die either way."

"What charge are you going to arrest me on?" Weston asked hoarsely. "You don't have any evidence."

"I have a witness who saw you shoot Red Sanders,"

Price said. "You'll hang, all right, and don't expect any help from the Mohawks. They're both dead." He paused, waiting for Weston fully to understand what that meant, then he added, "And don't expect any help from Barry Madden, either. He's seen the light."

Price was perfectly aware that he was playing a long shot. He wasn't sure Madden had seen the light, and he was even less sure that Bruce Jarvis would testify in court. If he didn't, taking Weston to the county seat was a waste of time.

He heard running steps on the boardwalk behind him, but he held his gaze on Weston. He heard Laura call, "Price! Price!" And Jean, "It's all right, Mr. Regan. Bruce promised me he'd testify against Weston."

Price swore under his breath. He needed this assurance, and he was glad Weston had heard it, but he didn't want them on the street now. Curly Blue, over on the far side, was edging away from the others. If Harker covered him, the rest of the Rocking C men would be free to go for their guns, and Price had to keep his gun on Weston.

Then Bruce Jarvis, scared and close to panic, cried out, "I seen you do it, Weston! I seen you shoot Red Sanders!"

Barry Madden, even now, could have tipped the scales and saved Cole Weston, but he didn't try. Maybe he had seen the light, as Price had said, or maybe he was afraid. Or perhaps it was Laura's presence here on the street. Now he shouted at her, "Inside. Come on, get inside."

Not much of a diversion, but enough for Curly Blue to make his play. He stood on the far side of the street, hand driving for gun butt and lifting the Colt from leather and swinging the barrel upward, a fast draw for a man who was not a professional, but slow compared to the draw Pete Nance had made.

Price cut him down with his first shot. Blue's knees buckled and he spilled forward into the dust; his gun dropped from his hand as he went down.

Harker yelled, "Stand pat! Morgan, get your hand away from your gun!"

Cole Weston wheeled and ran, head down, his long legs driving frantically toward the vacant lot between the jail and the building next to it. Price whirled toward him and threw a shot at his feet that kicked up dust. He shouted, "Hold it, Weston! Hold it!" But Weston reached the corner and disappeared.

Harker said, "Go get him, Regan. I'll keep these huckleberries right here."

Price raced across the front of the jail and turned the corner. Weston had almost reached the alley. Price fired and missed, the bullet knocking splinters from the corner of the jail. It was the last load in his gun. He yelled, "Hold it, Weston, or I'll shoot you in the back!"

Weston must have counted Price's shots. Gambling that there were only five, he reversed himself and whirled, drawing as he turned. Price lunged sideways and dropped on his face, rolling into the tall weeds alongside the jail.

Weston fired, his bullet lifting dust as it searched for Price. Desperately Price ejected the spent shells and reloaded as Weston ran toward him. Weston fired three more shots, the first two wide of the mark, the third slicing a ragged gouge in a board inches above Price's head.

For the first time in his life Cole Weston stood alone. He had no Pete Nance or Curly Blue to do his fighting for him, or even to back his play. Apparently that knowledge shattered his nerves, or those first two bullets would not have gone as wide as they had.

Price's fingers seemed to be all thumbs. Time had run out for him. Now Weston was close. He had stopped and was throwing down again. This time he couldn't miss. But the bullet didn't come. Someone yelled at him from the street. He stood motionless a second, his head up, his face twisted by a fury so violent and so terrible that he bore little resemblance to the self-confident Cole Weston Price had known.

Weston fired, but the bullet was not for Price. Whoever

had called from the street cried out in agony. Now
Price's gun was loaded. He lined it on Weston, calling,
"Get your hands up, Weston! Pronto!"

Price wanted to kill him. If a man ever deserved
killing, it was Cole Weston, but hanging was better, for it
would drive home a lesson to everyone on Elk River,
which sudden death from a bullet would fail to do.

Weston dropped his gun and lifted his hands. Price
marched him to the street, a whipped man for everyone
to see. Then Price saw that it was Bruce Jarvis who had
called and who had gone down before Weston's gun. He
lay on the walk, both hands clutching his thigh, blood
pouring between his fingers.

Already the doctor was on his way, black bag in hand.
Jean and Laura were running toward Bruce. There was
nothing Price could do for the boy at the moment.

Harker said, "Looks like it's finished. All right, gents,
start walking."

A moment later after the jail door had swung shut on
Weston and his men, Price said, "I'm going to get
something to eat and a fresh horse, Weston. I'm not
leaving you here for some of your men to bust you out
and have this to do all over again. Maybe you'll be able to
get word to your boys, but if you do and they start after
us, you'll be a dead man. I didn't shoot you a while ago
because I aim to see you hang, but I will shoot you before
I let you go."

He walked back to the office in the front of the
building. Barry Madden was not in sight. Price looked at
Harker. "I don't get it, Max, but I reckon you know what
you did. Words can't thank a man for saving . . ."

"Price, suppose you don't bother saying those words,"
Harker said. "For once in my life I feel like a man. It's
like I've told you; I've been dying for ten years, so it
didn't make much difference whether it was today or
tomorrow." He licked his lips, a finger scratching a
cherry-red cheek. "But I'll tell you one thing. I wouldn't
have done it, I guess, if it hadn't been for Laura. Treat her

good, Price. Always treat her good."

"You know I will, Max." Price laid his hand on the storekeeper's shoulder. "You've got a right to feel like a man, all the right in the world." He paused, then said, "Max, someone wrote to Ralph Carew . . ."

"I did," Harker interrupted. "I couldn't stand what Weston was doing." He nodded at the door. "Get out of here, you fool. Go find Laura."

Price went outside. The doctor had stopped the bleeding in Bruce's leg. He said, "You'll be all right, son. Just stay on your back for a few days. Be a spell before you do any walking."

"Take him to my house," Madden said. "Jean's staying there. She can take care of him."

Bruce looked at Price, his teeth clenched against the pain. "Regan," he said, "you figure I can look in the mirror now? Maybe be a little proud of what I see there?"

"You sure can," Price said. "Susie will be proud too. You'll see."

"Looked good, seeing Weston with his hands up," Bruce said. "Didn't figure it would ever happen."

"I didn't think you were seeing anything when Weston went past you," Price said.

"I seen that all right," Bruce said.

"Here's the stretcher." The doctor motioned the crowd back. "Ease him onto it, boys. Barney, you get hold of that end."

They carried him away, Jean walking beside the stretcher. The crowd moved off, leaving Barry Madden and Laura standing beside Price, Laura's hand on Price's arm.

Madden said, "I'll see you get the marshal's star back, Price. Might as well figure on getting married soon as you get back from the county seat. I'll buy that Bryce house and you and Laura can move right in."

Price looked at him contemptuously. Madden's side had lost. There had been a moment when he could have saved it, but cowardice had kept him from it, Price

thought, and not a change of heart. Now it was exactly
like him to swing to Price's side, to ignore what had
happened and try to take advantage of Laura's love for
Price.

"I think you've given your last order here," Price said.
"It's my guess you won't be in Saddle Rock much longer.
It's a cinch Laura and me won't be. I told you I was going
to run for sheriff when Carew's term is up."

He put an arm around Laura and swung her off the
walk. They moved away, leaving Barry Madden staring
after them. Price said, "Let's go to Grandma Spivey's
place and get something to eat. I've got to head out of
here with Weston as soon as I can."

Laura walked beside him, her arm through his. She
held her head high and proud, loving him and wanting
everybody who saw her to know it. Price was a little
proud, too. A man couldn't help it, with a girl like Laura
holding his arm and looking at him that way.

REAL WEST

The true life adventures of America's greatest frontiersmen.

THE LIFE OF KIT CARSON by John S.C. Abbott. Christopher "Kit" Carson could shoot a man at twenty paces, trap and hunt better than the most skilled Indian, and follow any trail — even in the dead of winter. His courage and strength as an Indian fighter earned him the rank of brigadier general of the U.S. Army. This is the true story of his remarkable life.

__2968-5 $2.95

THE LIFE OF BUFFALO BILL by William Cody. Strong, proud and courageous, Buffalo Bill Cody helped shape the history of the United States. Told in his own words, the real story of his life and adventures on the untamed frontier is as wild and unforgettable as any tall tale ever written about him.

__2981-2 $2.95